THE BLACK HORSE

D0291374

PS
8561
R38
P56
c.3

DISCARD
DISCARD

Date Due

0 5 MAR 1976			

REAL

PRINTED IN CANADA

FOR SHARON

ACKNOWLEDGMENTS
Journal of Canadian Fiction,
Tamarack Review, The Fiddlehead,
Ingluvin Magazine, Impulse
Intercourse, Tom Tom

INGLUVIN PUBLICATIONS,
P.O. Box 994, Place d'Armes Stn.,
Montreal 126, Canada

U.S. distribution: Ingluvin,
609 W 114th St., Suite 76,
New York, N.Y. 10025

Copyright   1972 by Raymond Fraser
ISBN 0 919522 73 4, paper
     0 919522 72 6, hardcover

Printed and bound in Canada.

Contents

They come here to die

1

SINCE THE BLACK Horse was the
only tavern in town it was not a good thing to get barred
from it if you were a man who liked to drink and socialize.
For about the hundredth time Ralph Ramsey was barred.
"This is it, Ralph, out you go! And this time it's final,
don't come back again." MacPherson the waiter escorted
him out the door and slammed it behind him and Ralph
staggered away in the night. For some reason his pal Danny
wasn't with him. It wasn't often they weren't together.
    "What'd he do this time, Mac?" I asked the waiter a few
days later.
    "Oh, he got up on the table ranting at everybody—'You're
all full of shit!' he says. 'You're nobodies! You're nothings!
What has any of you ever done, eh? Tell me that? What
kind of mark are you guys gonna leave behind when you're

dead? You're all full of shit!" You know what he gets like, the man's crazy, he should be put away."

Other times Ralph had been barred for bumming money around the tables, or fighting, or playing his trumpet, or breaking glasses, or any combination of these things. His friend Danny had been barred with him a few times, but Danny was not so unpredictable, he was less given to explosive outbursts. By himself it's unlikely he'd have been barred more than a few times.

A couple of weeks later, in the normal course of events, the two of them would drift in the door and sit quietly in the corner. "Okay if we have a drink, MacPherson? We just dropped in for a quick one."

MacPherson was by nature a kind and easygoing man, and by this time would have forgiven or forgotten about the last incident, and he'd serve them like any other customers in good standing.

Although it may sound like Ralph was a wildman, he wasn't. He was only that way sometimes, when he had too much to drink, and even then only when the mood struck him. Otherwise, drunk or sober, he was a sensitive and thoughtful person. It would be hard to say his age, he was one of those individuals who seemed to have always been around Newbridge, a fixture like the Black Horse itself, or the town hall, or the Catholic church. He may have been forty, perhaps not much more than thirty-five. Then again he might have been forty-five. He had a moustache and a closely-cropped beard and thick hair that poured down over his collar. This was in the early sixties and Ralph's appearance was then considered rather eccentric, as was his general behaviour.

One day, in fact it was the afternoon of Christmas day, he dropped in to my place while I was doing the dishes. It was a freezing wintry day but he had no coat on. He looked haggard. "I didn't sleep at all last night," he said, taking a seat at the kitchen table. "I can't sleep anymore. I never could. I don't know what's wrong with me. I walk around all night and then when daylight comes I go to bed. When everyone else's getting up I'm turning in. Yes, I walk all night. The cops are starting to look at me. One of these days they're going to arrest me."

"Arrest you? What for?"

"I don't know, for something, for impersonating a human being." He had a laugh at that.

It being Christmas there was a bottle of rye sitting on the table. Ralph eyed it a few minutes, then said, "You don't mind if I have a taste of that."

"Here." I poured him a drink.

"That's nice stuff. Very smooth. Did you get that for Christmas?"

"Yeah. From myself."

"I got some liquor too. I mean my mother did. No, I guess it was me. I was at home last night and there were gifts under the tree, and I thought, this must be mine, *Evening in Paris*, so I drank that. Yeah, I got lots of booze. It's all gone now, I drank it last night. The old lady doesn't know yet. *My Sin*, that's another one. *Chanel No. 5*. One of these days I'll go into some posh bar, I'll be standing there looking sophisticated, and the bartender'll say, 'What's yours? What're you gonna have?' 'Oh, I guess I'll have an *Evening in Paris*. On the rocks.' It's so long since I had the real stuff I forget what it's called. Shaving lotion, vanilla extract, rubbing alcohol—perfume! As long as it comes in a bottle that's the important thing. You can't drink the labels."

He'd brought his trumpet with him, which was about the only thing he owned, aside from his clothes. "I want to play you a number," he said. "Something in season." So he played *Adeste fideles* and almost blew the ceiling off the kitchen. In a small room like my kitchen it sounded

very loud. Whether he was a good player or not I don't
know, sometimes he seemed extremely gifted and other
times not so good. I think it depended on the mood he was
in. He had been playing the trumpet for years and years,
ever since he was a boy. Several times he attempted to
play with local bands but it never worked out. He couldn't
read music and he had his own ideas about arrangements,
and he had difficulty keeping sober. He was, you might
say, a musician who relied on inspiration, and his
temperament made it difficult for him to adjust to other
musicians and regular dates. There were two local groups
that played places like Saturday night dances at the
Legion, skatingnights at the rink, at the Air Cadets'
annual dance, and for formal highschool dances. Ralph
claimed they were mediocre musicians who followed
unimaginative arrangements, and I would say he was
right. So Ralph played for himself and for friends and at
the yearly Sanatorium Club amateur night where he was a
big hit but never received a prize.

"Thank you, Ralph, that was very nice," I said.

"I lost my teeth last night. I had all my teeth pulled a
while back and got a plate. But I left my coat somewhere
and my teeth were in the pocket. Yes, Dr. Reeves pulled
all my teeth out and he was going to give me a plate. I
said to him, why don't you throw in a cup and saucer while
you're at it, a plate's no good by itself. This is great
stuff. You don't mind if I have another one?" I poured him
another rye. I remember Ralph saying once he'd gone to a
doctor because he thought he had ulcers, and the doctor
wanted to know about his drinking habits. "He gave me
this test, it was a list of twenty questions to find out if
someone's an alcoholic, and if you answered yes to two of
them that meant you were. There were things like, Do you
drink because you feel shy with other people, Do you crave
a drink in the morning, Do you drink to escape worries or

troubles—there were twenty of them, and I answered yes to them all—except one. And that was, Does your drinking interfere with your job? I put down no for that one." Ralph hadn't had a job in ten years.

Ralph took a pull on his glass of rye. He sat there a moment silently. When he spoke his voice sounded very sad. "No work, no money, no women, nothing. I've got the feeling I'm just watching life go by and I can't do a thing about it.' He shook his head. "I came here to play a song and have a few drinks and be happy, but it's no good. You know, everybody around this town thinks I'm a bum. Everybody does. I can't get a girl. Not a chance. You want to know something that happened? I asked a girl out a couple of weeks ago. I said, how'd you like to go out with me some night. Do you know what she said? She said, I wouldn't go to the shithouse with you. How would you like it if a girl said that to you? That's pretty bad, eh? A girl has no right to say that to a man, no matter who she is or what she thinks of you. But that's my status around here. Just because I don't have a job and live like everyone else. I'm an individual. I don't have to do what everyone wants me to do. I may not have much in this life but I've got my own mind. What I should do is get out of here. Why don't I get out? Tell me that?"

"I don't know. It's up to you."

"I guess so." He was quiet again. Then he said, "Well, I'll have to go home and see my mother and father. Then it's back to my own estate on Water street. My parents, they watch me like two cats to see I don't step out of line. But I'm always drunk just the same. I've got nothing else to do. I'm an alcoholic. I can prove it, just ask me twenty questions. I drink and I don't do anything else."

"How much do you drink anyway, Ralph?"

"How much? As much as I can get. I'd be drinking twenty-four hours a day if I could afford it. But I've got no money. I'm living on welfare. Did you know that? Me, on welfare. What do you think of that? I get sixty dollars a month. I give my mother and father forty-five and I keep the rest. So I have to go bumming on the streets to get enough for a drink. That's how low I've come. I bum money down on the front street. A bum." He got to his feet, still holding his glass with an inch of rye in it. "I have to try and find my coat. My scarf is in the pocket, and my teeth. But I don't care about the teeth. I hardly ever wear them anyway."

"They must make eating easier."

"No, I don't eat with them. They aren't comfortable. They're just decorations. I only wear them at special times, like when someone asks me out." He laughed. "Yeah, when I'm asked out, that's the only time I wear them. Anyway, I've got to get going. What time is it now? I'm going blind, I can't even see that clock there."

"It's twenty-to-five."

"There, I'm late already." He emptied his glass and at the door shouted over his shoulder, "Merry Christmas and a happy New Year!"

There was one detail about Ralph's visit that I didn't pay attention to. Shortly before leaving he went to the bathroom. When he came out he didn't stay around much longer. I learned why the following afternoon.

Ralph was at the door and came sheepishly in. "The thief returns to the scene of the crime," he said.

"Yeah?" I didn't know what he meant.

"Ah me. I'm cold sober. I woke up this morning ready to put down a big drink of rum, I'd had it hid away under the bed, and I was thinking by God it's good to have a drink in the morning, I need one real bad, and I've got a pint of rum sitting there under the bed. A pint of rum!" And he started laughing to himself. "Yes, that's the way to start the day. I had it all figured out, I didn't touch the pint last night, saving it for the morning so I could start the day off right. Well, that's what you get. Crime doesn't pay! Yes, the thief returns to the scene of the crime."

"What're you talking about, Ralph?"

"Have you got a beer? You wouldn't have a beer in the house?"

It being the season the fridge was stocked, so I got out a couple of pints of Moosehead.

"Ah that feels good, nice and cold. Yes sir, I unscrewed the cap and was set to bolt down a big drink the first thing in the morning. By God it's a good thing I didn't. Turpentine. That's the way to start the day—with a good shot of turpentine. Here I thought I had a nice pint of rum and it was turpentine."

Now I understood. My bathroom was quite a mess, and among other things lying around were several bottles of turpentine which I used for cleaning paint brushes. If you didn't know what it was you'd think they were bottles of booze, because I had the stuff in rum bottles. Ralph had spotted them when he went to take a leak and thought it was the real thing.

"You mean—you stole one of those bottles—"

"That's right. Ah, what a person I am, I've got no scruples, I come here and drink your liquor and then try to steal more of it. I must have no shame, no conscience at all. I hated to do it. But I saw those bottles there and I thought this is just what I need for the morning. Perfume in the evening and the real stuff in the morning. I got up and reached for the bottle this morning with hands trembling and I took the cap off and started to take a drink. That's what I get. Turpentine! It's punishment for my sins."

Well, we laughed a bit at that and drank a lot of beer. At some stage in the afternoon Ralph once again bemoaned the fact that he was reduced to nothing but a bum and an alcoholic. "I went to the AA's for a while," he said, "I tried to kick the habit. But that's no good. They can't help me. I remember one meeting, you know the way these things go, this guy got up on the platform telling us his life story, what hell his life was when he was drinking and why he had to stop. I don't even know his name, he was some guy from upriver, I never saw him before. This was the first night that Jackie Craig, it was the only night, somebody had persuaded Jackie to go to the meeting and he was standing there at the back of the room, you could tell he was skeptical and reluctant, and this fellow up on the stage was saying how when he drank he used to beat his wife and children, really kick them around, punch them silly, little kids and all. He was giving a big description of these things, these terrible things he used to do, and he was going on and on about it, and all of a sudden there was this disgusted voice from the back of the room: 'You're not an alcoholic, you're *nuts*!' That was Jackie. Soon as he said that he turned and walked out."

It was fall, late October, this particular time Ralph got barred from the Black Horse. Being barred wasn't all that much an inconvenience, there were plenty of places to drink so long as you could come up with the price of a bottle. Ralph's own room, for example, in the old Kelly rooming house by the ferry wharf—a place he despised—or up at the racetrack in the brokendown grandstand (no races were held there anymore and the track was overrun with weeds), or the ballpark, or down on the station wharf, or in one of the boxcars at the CN station, or behind one of the stores on Water street where the ground was covered with broken wine and rum bottles. But in the cold weather it was better to be indoors, and in the Black Horse there was always someone there and Ralph enjoyed company.

Most of the time his company was Danny Sullivan. Danny was quite a bit younger than Ralph, he was then about twenty-two or twenty-three. He had left school at the age

of sixteen after several years of trying to surmount the
eighth grade, and in the six or so years since then he had
not been employed very much. A day in Danny's life can
be described simply enough.

He lived with his parents and around noon he would rise
and eat a couple of strips of raw bacon washed down with
coke, then shuffle down the road to the pool hall. He would
spend the afternoon shooting pool or playing the pinball
machines or watching others do these two things. If
someone came up with a bottle of something he probably
wouldn't go home for supper. If not he would go home and
eat, not saying a word to his mother and father. They had
stopped saying words to him as well, after years of talking
at deaf ears. The only exception was once every two or
three months when there would be a row over his not
getting a job. This accomplished nothing and another
several months of silence followed. His father had got him
work once as a house painter but Danny lasted only to his
first pay check, which he blew in two nights of unparalleled
generosity towards his friends. This brought him to the
realization that working didn't pay—not two weeks of
backbreaking work for a two night drunk—so he neglected
to return to the job on Monday, or ever after.

After supper it was down town again where he inevitably
met Ralph on the street. If there was any money they pooled
it and caught the liquor store before it closed. If there was
none or not enough they spent the next few hours bumming,
or they hunted around to find someone who would buy a
bottle for the pleasure of their company, usually some raw
teenager. Then they made for one of the many bootleggers
in town.

When the night ended Danny went home to bed. Every day
it was more or less the same story.

Danny was Ralph's close associate for several reasons.
One, he had the same amount of time on his hands; two, he

had an attraction to the bottle; three, he was a misfit and knew it, just like Ralph; four, he wasn't, despite his limited education, all that stupid and Ralph could talk to him; five, they shared a fervent dislike for the town and almost everyone in it.

2

The night after Ralph was barred from the Black Horse for his tirade from the tavern table he was down in his room by the ferry wharf. It was a miserable rainy October night, the kind of cold rain that hits your skin like frozen needles. Ralph's room was on the second floor at the back corner of the building. It had two windows, one facing the river and the other looking down on the lane leading from Water street to the ferry slip. There was a streetlight at the lane corner and at intervals sheets of water gusted past the light. Except for the weather outside this could be any night of the year. Ralph was standing looking out the window, hands behind his back. Behind him lying on the sunken bed with both shoes planted firmly on the blankets was Danny. "What're we gonna do?" said Danny, for about the half-dozenth time.

"I don't know, we can't go out in this. Why don't you go up to the tavern."

"The hell with that. If they won't let *you* in, the hell with them. They're not gonna get my business. Besides all I got is a quarter. We could go up to the Castle." The Castle was a restaurant, a teenage hangout where they did much of their panhandling.

"Won't be anyone there tonight. Only a crazy person would be out on a night like this. It wouldn't be worth the walk."

When they were silent you could hear the rain, and from
a room above a record was playing "I Walked in the
Garden with Jesus." When it reached the end whoever was
playing it started it over again. The same hymn had been
repeating itself now for over half an hour.

"You know, that could drive you crazy," said Danny
staring up at the ceiling. "Who lives up there anyway?"

"I don't know, I don't know *anybody* in this place.
They're all old people," said Ralph. "I'm the only one
here under eighty. I don't know where they all come from.
I see them creeping up and down the stairs and along the
halls. They just look at you but they never say anything."

Danny fished a package of tobacco from his back pocket.
He rolled a cigaret and the shredded end flamed briefly
when he lit it. "Be great to have a drink now," he said.

"I'm glad you came over," said Ralph, still staring out
the window. He shook his head. "What a goddamn dismal
depressing sight. I can't stand being alone in this room
anymore, I'd rather be in jail. At least you'd know why
you're there. I'm serving a sentence and I haven't been
arrested yet. Solitary confinement. It's nice to get a
visitor."

"I don't blame you. I couldn't take this place very long
myself," said Danny. Ralph's room, it was true, didn't
have much to recommend it. It was like a large box with
brownish wallpaper on it and yellow stains seeping down
from the ceiling. The ceiling itself was a network of cracks
and places where the plaster had fallen revealing wooden
slats. The furniture was a bed, a wooden chair, a small
chest of drawers and a table which was now covered with
dirty dishes and utensils. The lightbulb was weak giving
the place a dusky atmosphere. There was no heat and both
of them kept their coats on.

"Well, what'll we do?" said Ralph.

"Play something why don't you. Anything to drown out

that noise upstairs."

Ralph took his trumpet out of its dog-eared leather case. Different times he'd been on the verge of selling it, feeling there was no important reason for keeping it, he wasn't going anywhere, but each time he hadn't been able to go through with it. He knew that once gone it was unlikely he'd ever get the money together to buy it back or get another one.

"What do you want?"

"Play *Ruby*."

Ralph blew on the trumpet but his heart wasn't in it. He stopped after a short while. "I don't feel like it. I'll play it later."

"That was good, that sounded real good. I wish to hell I could play a trumpet like that, or anything, even a mouth-organ."

"Well, you're not too bad a singer. That's enough."

"Yeah, I can sing, I'm not a bad singer. Maybe we should form a group, just the two of us. We might go places."

Ralph paced the short distance across the room and back.

"It's going to be another goddamn cold winter. You know they don't have any heat in this building? If you want heat you have to buy your own heater. Last winter—it was like a refrigerator in here last winter. I can't afford a heater. There should be a law against this, it's no way for a man to live. It might be all right for an Eskimo. But I'm not an Eskimo."

"You can already see your breath."

"And look at these, storm windows they call them, they're supposed to keep out the cold. French safes, they stretch big French safes across the windows and leave them on all year and you're protected from the cold." There were plastic coverings over the windows, they had stretched and sagged and they flapped in the wind and distorted the view

outside. "You can't take your clothes off in the winter, I
went months and I couldn't take my clothes off for fear of
dying of exposure. I wasn't warm one minute for more than
six months. That's a helluva way to live. I don't want
another winter in this hole. I'd rather live in an igloo. What
I should do is make myself an igloo this winter and live in
that. Even an Eskimo wouldn't live under these conditions."

"At least it's a place to have a drink, it's a good thing
they don't bother you that way."

"That's true."

"If we *had* a drink. We should get a quart of wine. How're
we gonna get a quart of wine?"

They heard the sound of slow feet shuffling in the hall,
passing the door and ascending the stairs. They listened
until the footsteps were gone.

"Another old man," muttered Ralph. "This house is full
of old men, they all come here to die. I shouldn't be here.
I'm not an old man. I don't belong here."

He picked up his trumpet and blew a deafening defiant
blast. A sharp knocking sounded on the wall.

"Who's that?" said Danny.

"Another old man. Or maybe it's an old woman. They
don't like to hear me playing at night—or anytime for that
matter. They want to die quietly."

"What we need—we gotta get out of here, that's what,"
said Danny. "I mean out of town. We're both wasting our
talents here, especially you, not so much me since I don't
have any, but I'm getting sick of this place. I'll never get
anywhere in a dump like this. We should just get up and
get the hell out, just like that. No wasting time."

"Where would we go?"

"Anywhere. Montreal. No, Toronto'd be better, Montreal's
full of crazy Frenchmen, we'd never get along. Toronto."

"You can't go anywhere without money. How would we
get there? What would we live on?"

"It wouldn't take much. I could probably steal enough off the old man. We get a train up then we get a job, we'd soon be living pretty good. The booze is cheaper too. Lots of broads around, be no problem."

"I don't know anything about Toronto. They'd never give me a job. A guy my age."

"Look, you play the trumpet, eh? There are hundreds of bands in Toronto, they're always looking for talent. Look, Ralph, for Christsake, you can't wait forever. I mean, around here they don't know a trumpet from a shoe horn— you're crazy hanging around Newbridge."

"I know, I know." Ralph pondered a moment. "Yes, you're right. I have to get out of here, that's the only solution. I can't just sit around this town and die." A moment later he said, "Ah, it's no use. We'd never make it. You need money, you need connections, we'd be lost in Toronto."

"C'mon, don't talk like that. I thought you wanted to leave."

"Sure. Sure I want to leave."

Danny got up off the bed and with a long snorting snuffle inhaled his nose clean and spit into the grocery bag Ralph was using for garbage. "Well, make up your mind. I'm ready to go."

"I don't think you are, Danny. If I said, okay, let's pack, you'd make up some excuse for putting it off."

"No I wouldn't." He settled himself back on the bed.

"You know, the worst thing is they don't give you a chance," said Ralph. The wind and rain were shaking the plastic storm windows, snapping them against the inside windows. "They're only interested in themselves. Well, I don't give a shit about them. Who are they anyway? They're a bunch of nobodies."

"The hell with everybody," said Danny.

"All they want to do is push you into the dirt, they aren't satisfied unless you're crawling in front of them."

"It's no good talking about it. My Christ I wish we had something to drink, I'm croaking. I should've asked the old man for a few bucks." He adjusted the pillow under his head. "But I wouldn't give the bastard the satisfaction."

"It's not that I'm not good enough. It's not that."

"You're *too* good for them. They can't stand that."

"I just don't get a chance. I'm getting old, I'm an old man now."

"C'mon, Ralph, you're not old. You're a young man. You got a lot of time left and you got the talent. What've I got?"

"Pass me your tobacco."

Ralph rolled a cigaret and lit a match with his thumbnail. He dragged on the cigaret and fingered his beard. "I think I'll shave this off," he said.

"What?"

"The beard. I'm going to shave it tomorrow."

"How come? It looks good. Don't be crazy."

"I don't care. I need a change. Maybe I'll try and get a job. That'd be a change, I mean if I can get a job."

"Maybe I should get one too."

"But who'll hire us? They think we're bums."

"The hell with them."

"No, it's no good. Maybe if I shave nobody will know me. They might hire me that way. I could say I'm a stranger in town. What d'you think?"

"The hell with them. The best thing to do is get up to Toronto. There's no future hanging around here. I could be your manager." He flipped his butt towards the garbage bag. It hit the side and rolled back a few inches towards the bed.

"Yeah, my manager. That's what I need, a manager. Okay, you're now my manager."

"How much of a cut do I get?"

"I'll give you fifty per cent. How's that sound? Fifty per cent of nothing."

"No, I'm serious."

"Okay, I'll pay you in advance. How about . . . " He reached in his pocket and pulled out a ball of paper which he opened. It was a two dollar bill. "How about fifty per cent of a bottle of wine."

"Hey! Where'd you get that?" said Danny. "Here we've been sitting around here—"

"I got it from my father to buy a pair of gloves for the winter. I was up to see him this afternoon. But I don't need gloves, it's not my hands that need to get warm. I can always keep my hands in my pockets. I'd only lose a pair of gloves anyway."

"How come you didn't tell me? I mean we been sitting here—"

"I don't know. I was just thinking . . . "

"Give it to me. I'll go over to Nose's and get a bottle."

"No, I'll go with you, I don't want to stay here, I'm sick of this room. I'd rather be out in the rain than here."

Ralph pulled the string in the light and they went out into the hall. The hall was musty smelling and the only light was from the ground floor below. They went by a shadow standing at the head of the stairs, they could hear him breathing, one of the old men who lived in the house.

"This place gives me the creeps," Danny muttered going down the stairs.

Water was streaming over the street and the rain hit them like icicles. All the way up Water street there wasn't a soul in sight, it was like a ghost town. The wind whipped the rain at them.

"Where we gonna go once we get it?" said Danny. "We can't stay out in this." They walked along quickly with hands in pockets and shoulders hunched into the rain.

"We can sit in a boxcar."

"It's kinda cold."

"A few drinks and we'll be all right."

"Yeah."

The Quebec Prison

FLIGHT FROM MONTREAL

HAVE YOU HEARD this one? About the major league ball player who thought he could sing? He put a record out and it was a dismal failure. Naturally he was quite annoyed and he began complaining to his agent, and his agent, a philosophical man, said: "Oh well, you can always go for a walk."

"A walk?"

"Sure. A walk's as good as a hit."

Yes, I know, that's not much of a joke, even if you're familiar with baseball expressions. All the same I get a slight charge out of it. The reason is, I made it up by myself. Like an after-dinner speaker I wanted to start off with a joke, something to catch your interest and put you in a pleasant, hence vulnerable mood.

I invented one other joke and I might have opened with it but I was told it wasn't original. The truth is, it *was* original, it was original with me, and the fact another person also thought it up is simply a coincidence. I can see why this happened because it's quite an obvious piece of wit.

The famous newspaper tycoon Lord Thompson was in Montreal for a few days—this is the joke here—and when he left a fellow says to his friend: "I hear Thompson bought the Montreal *Star* while he was in town."

"What? How much did he pay for it?"

"Ten cents."

I like to pretend I'm creative and a man of great potential. If you have never produced very much in the way of art it's important to believe in your poetential. Observe. I made a typing error and produced a new word, "poetential". By accident I have just described myself perfectly, since I have for some time considered myself a poet and have been meaning for years to write some very good verse.

Generally I'm an accurate speller, that word, as I said, was a slip of the typewriter. Some poets are atrocious spellers. There have always been poor spellers in the world of literature. One day not so long ago I was in the Montreal Public Library reading some books on witchcraft and it was quite a difficult task. I copied down a few passages which will give you an idea of what I mean.

"Alison Peirson was conuict of the vsing of Sorcerie and Witchcraft, with the Inuocation of the spreitis of the Deuill; speciallie in the uisioune and forme of ane Mr. William Sympsoune, hir cousing and moder-brotheris-sone, quha sche affirmit wes ane grit scoller and doctor of medicin . . .

"The deuell was cled in ane blak goun with ane blak hat vpon his head . . . his faice was terrible, his noise lyk the bek of ane egle, great bournyng eyn; his handis and leggis

were ĥerry, with clawes vpon his handis, and feit lyk the
griffon."

The author of that must have given his teachers fits while
at school. The spelling! There was also a good recipe in
the book, used by the witches on special occasions. I don't
remember it all but I remember this line " . . . a pairt
of the head, a pairt of the buttocks, and they made a py
thereof . . ." The husband, as he comes in the door, holl-
ers: *What's for dessert tonight, dear?* "How abovt ane peece of py?"

I didn't find any answers in witchcraft so I go on daydream-
ing of extreme and violent deeds to rid the world of its evil.

Living in a city the size of Montreal is no joke. I don't
understand how the other citizens tolerate it. But they don't
seem to mind. It's the noise that gets me. Well, I realize
there are others who are bothered too but we're a minority.
It was sometime in May, a man in his undershirt was
hammering away fixing his shabby rotten back balcony. Each
blow of the hammer was like a cannon going off in a cave,
the sound was confined and magnified by the brick walls of
the backyards. It was a very hot day, so hot that I couldn't
close the windows or I'd suffocate. The hammering went
on. It was like living inside a throbbing toothache or a
pounding headache. I·got up, paced furiously back and forth,
then ran outside. Cars were roaring along the street with
horns honking and tires squealing, there were volleys of
motorcycles, salvos of heavy trucks, ambulances with sirens
screaming. Then thundering above a jet airliner passed
over low on its way to landing. When it died away a helicopter appeared, the CJAD traffic helicopter guiding cars to
and fro on the city arteries, a headnumbing stuttering
clattering of blades. Ah me, sometimes I accomodate myself,
I speak to myself and say: "*This* is the city. When you live
in the city this is what you hear. It is not your city, it
belongs to others, to those who like it this way. To real
city people these sounds are music in their ears, just as the

vile air is perfume to their noses, and cement and glass
canyons are artistic monuments to man's scope and
ingenuity, and crowded sweaty streets display the pride of
numbers. All these things are the city. The city is *not* quiet
fields where you can hear the wind. It is not little brooks
rippling, it is not the fresh scent of pine needles. It is not
a sky awash with diamond stars at night, nor the song of
crickets, it is not peace and serenity, things do not move
leisurely. No, that is the country. So do not confuse the city
with the country. If you don't like it here, leave. *But I can't
afford to.* Get some money then. Meanwhile, as you are a
guest of the city do not try to make it into something it
isn't. For one reason, you can't, and trying will only cause
frustration and lead to hardening of your arteries and probably insanity. Don't jump when you hear taxis blast their
horns for no good reason. You know that in the city taxi
drivers operate their cabs with one hand always on the horn.
Don't jump and look and say, "Why'd he do that?" and then
give him the finger and yell out at him, "Fucking idiot!"
so that the city dwellers around you look at you as if you're
crazy. The taxi driver doesn't hear you anyway because he's
too occupied racing around the streets in a steaming sweat
trying to make his eight dollars a day. Montreal has more
taxis per population than any other city in North America.
If you stand on a downtown street you will find more than
half the vehicles that go by are taxis. 75% of the horns that
are honked are the work of taxi drivers, although there are
many, many other drivers who do the same. You could, of
course, blame the auto makers who seem to take pains to
make horns as loud and nerve piercing as possible. But then
auto makers are city people, and they wouldn't understand
if you protested. Protesting only leads to ulcers unless you
have the temperament for it. *Some* people could not live
happily *without* protesting. They are very valuable members
of any community, they are more important than priests,

politicians, lawyers, teachers, generals, businessmen,
policemen, doctors. They are the most important people of
all because they try to check the human animal's boundless
and shortsighted rapacity. I mean in particular those who
are fighting noise and other man-made products of commerce.
They are good and important people. But you, my friend, you
aren't one of them. Hence taking on the job of destroying a
city the size of Montreal would be frustratingly impossible,
not to say thankless."

So, in summary, my voice's advice was to accept the city
while living in it, and leave when I could, but not permit
myself to lose my sanity because above all there is one
important person in the world and that is me. You may say
the same about yourself. It is a simple but sad truth and it
is why everyone, for instance, is aware that the internal
combustion engine causes dangerous problems but very few
are willing to give up the one they own. It's really the *other*
ones, after all, everybody should give up his car and then
there would be only my car, and one car doesn't cause
enough contamination to bother a fly.

This hot sunshiny day in May I began to shudder, my
stomach sunk horribly into a cringing little bladder, my
nervous system began to scream, I had not time to go through
my rationalizing sermon, to calm myself. I knew I had to get
away, if only for a while. I grabbed a train for Quebec City.

Quebec is a city, it's true, but it's a much smaller city
and its old town is so like old Europe that the mere sight of
it is soothing. And a change, wherever you go, is always a
balm to the nerves, unless you go someplace like jail,
which is where I landed shortly, then it's a change for the
worse.

Another reason I went to Quebec was I had a friend there,
and that meant a place to stay.

When travelling on a train the feel of the wheels, the rhythm of the wheels invariably draws melodies out of me, new melodies never before heard. Someday I'll take a tape recorder with me and hum my melodies into it. Then I'll have proof that I am a musically creative person.

I sat by the window and on the empty seat beside me was my bottle of wine, in a brown paper bag. It was a cheap sherry, called *Normandie*, but it tasted good, and they make it in New Brunswick—the province I grew up in and possibly the reason I am not a city person and never will be, despite living in places like Montreal and Toronto for five or six years. You pay more for the same wine in New Brunswick, but then New Brunswick is a poorer province and there are more winos per capita there. Some day I'll study economics.

It's a pleasure to sit on a train and sip wine. Sometimes you have to compromise with your ideals, unless you're an extreme purist which I am not quite. I used a paper cup, a disposable cup, to drink my wine from, since it would not have looked proper tipping the bottle back, not to mention there was the possibility of the conductor seeing me.

With my shoes off I leaned back and watched the country-side roll by. On a sunny afternoon in May the fields and trees were fresh and vibrantly green. We passed farms with large silos and cows in the fields; we went through little towns, raced through without stopping, French names on the stores, the little balconied hotels, the local taverns, the impressive stone churches; for while we ran parallel to a highway and I shook my fists at the cars streaming silently along, their noise locked out by the windows of the train and its own clippeting wheels. But I was feeling better, the travelling made me feel better, along with the wine and the sense of escaping from Montreal, and it wasn't long before we pulled into Quebec.

I know there is no other city in North America like
Quebec, the old part that is, the walled city and Lower
Town. The newer part which sprawls back from the river and
up and down is like your average urban mess. And in the
old city there are a number of those giant windowed boxes
which go under the name of modern city architecture. It
amuses me, in an unamusing way, when I look at the Royal
Victoria Hospital in Montreal. Half it is old and charming,
something like the buildings on the Royal Way in Edinburgh,
in fact it looks something like Scottish castle. The other
half was built recently. I picture in my mind the architect
saying, when it was decided to build additions to the
hospital, standing before the Board of Governors: "I have
the perfect design, Gentlemen, a beautiful design, nothing
like the ugly antiquated structures you now have. My design,
ah, it's breathtaking, the lines, the beauty, it's the height
of architectural artistry!" And the governors of course are
eager to see a model, but the architect says he forgot to
bring it with him. "However, one moment, Gentlemen." And
he steps out into the hall and goes to the incinerator room
and comes back with a discarded cardboard packing box.
"Now." And taking a pen he draws little squares on the
sides of the box, identical rows and rows of them, and when
finished says: "There. Magnificent! Behold your new buildings." And so they were built and they're there today.
    Despite some, as they say, progressive demolition and
construction the old city of Quebec still resembles an old
city in Europe, it looks much like it did hundreds of years
ago when it was built with care and skill, and it has been
preserved, buildings restored, conveniences and luxuries
added inside but the exteriors kept to the same appearance.
The streets are cobblestoned and narrow and rarely follow a
straight line. If it weren't for the inevitable congestion of
automobiles you could easily walk around the city feeling
like an old musketeer.

My friend Bernard lived on Rue Leclerc. He had a large bright room on the second floor of a solid old stone building on the hill. He had a gabled window, and the slanting roof on the street side of his room gave it the appearance of an artist's studio, the traditional attic kind. Bernard was an artist of sorts, he worked with leather. He made belts, sandals, purses, jackets, vests, even pants. In Montreal he had sold his work to boutiques. I myself still wear a wide belt that he made and sold to me. In Quebec, though, he didn't try to do any selling because it would not have been wise, since he was in the act of hiding out from the police.

Bernard answered my ring and let me in with a smile. He was almost always smiling, a tiny secret smile as though he knew something that no one else did, and perhaps that was true. I followed him up the narrow flight of stairs to his room. It hadn't been easy to find his place because I was reluctant to ask directions, being not at all fluent in French. And I knew from previous visits to Quebec that English is virtually an unknown language there. I had wandered around a while, reading all the street signs, trying to find it on my own. Once while in Quebec, my first time there, I suffered an embarrassment. Just off the train I went into the first tavern I saw and said to myself, "Now that I'm in Quebec I'm going to act like a Frenchman." So when the waiter came I said, "Un gros Dow, s'il vous plait." What could be simpler than that? I'd heard it hundreds of times in Montreal taverns. But the waiter, without moving away, said something to me. I hadn't the faintest notion what he was saying, so I repeated, "Gros Dow, un gros Dow." Then he repeated what he had said, which was gibberish to me. I became slightly flustered, because I knew that he now knew that I had been bluffing, that I couldn't speak French at all. I said, "Dow, gros Dow?" sort of

feebly. What had I done wrong? He gave me a look as much
as to say I was a stupid ass and went and got me the beer.
In a hurry to get out of there I drank it quickly. But before
leaving I believe I deduced what he'd been saying. I saw
him bring a beer off the shelf rather than out of the cooler
to another customer. Thus he must have wanted to know if
I preferred my beer cold or off the shelf. Nobody ever asked
me that in Montreal.

I stopped a kindly looking old man on the street and said,
"Pardon, où est Rue Leclerc?" My pronunciation was very
bad because he had me repeat it three or four times. Then
his face brightened and he began pouring out the French,
none of which I could decipher, and pointing. I said, "Merci,"
and went off in the direction he'd indicated with his finger.
One more such encounter, this time with an attractive girl
(since I had to ask *somebody*), of which there are many in
Quebec, brought me to Rue Leclerc and Bernard's address.

Bernard is a tall and athletic looking fellow. In Montreal
he had worn an enormous mop of bushy brown hair but for
what I assumed to be purposes of disguise it was now
trimmed down to where it was almost short. For the same
reason he was in the process of growing a moustache.

I respected and admired Bernard, he was a man dedicating
his life to a dangerous and important mission, and it had
already got him in trouble. About a year ago he had read
somewhere, in some radical newspaper it would have been,
a letter proposing a scheme for destroying what is sometimes referred to as the car culture. He showed me the letter
which he had clipped out. It wasn't long and I can remember
the wording more or less. It went like this.

Dear Editor:
   What is one of the biggest problems in the North
American industrialized consumer-oriented society?
The automobile, which kills and maims by collisions

and smog, fills the air with noise (as well as fumes),
dictates and disfigures the layout of cities and country-
side—there is nothing good about it, except its speed
which should only be necessary in times of emergency.
For transportation subways and electric trains and
buses are the answer. Also bicycles. Even a return
to horses.

Cars are a perfect object for guerilla attack. Carry
a bag of sugar wherever you go and whenever the
opportunity arises dump some in the gas tank of a car.
Each guerilla should set a goal of a thousand cars
knocked out. Fight against the death-dealing and
environment disfiguring machine. Exempt only
ambulances and fire engines.

Yours for survival
The Sugar Man

"When I read it," Bernard said to me, "I realized I'd found
what I was looking for. That letter said it all. That was it
right there. I'd been casting around, wondering what to do,
seeing the world go up in fumes, people thrown out of their
low-cost houses to make room for inner city expressways,
historical buildings torn down, life becoming a nightmare
of engine noises and smells and sights. It was eating me
up inside. Yes, that's what it was doing. I had marched in
demonstrations, collected petitions, written letters, wore
my STOP THE HIGHWAY button. But it didn't help at all,
or hardly at all. Then I read that letter and I couldn't get
it out of my mind. I knew what I had to do."

So he started doing what the Sugar Man, whoever he might
be, advised. He began going about at night and slipping
sugar into gas tanks. He made a point of picking out those
heavy, powerful racing-type sports cars which a lot of young
men affect on the road, the ones with the wide wheels and
the huge loud engines and usually with a few decals on

them, like "STP" or the *Playboy* bunny. But if he couldn't
find one of these he went for Cadillacs and large Buicks
and Oldsmobiles and Chryslers. As a last resort he would
knock out a smaller vehicle.

He had gotten to more than a hundred cars when one
careless or unlucky night in March he found himself in the
glare of a policeman's flashlight. I mentioned that Bernard
looked like an athlete but he more than looked it, he was
strong and fast, and was able to elude this cop in the dark—
after kicking him severely in the groin—and there was quite
a hunt on for him, and the story appeared in the papers.
Feeling it was the wise thing to do he fled the city for
Quebec. Unlike myself he could speak some French, enough
to get by on satisfactorily.

He called me up one day telling me where he was, asking
me to come visit him sometime because he knew no one in
Quebec. He spent his time working with leather, and also
did some metalwork, like making medallions, and he was
working on some soapstone carvings as well. He was a
tireless, deliberate and talented craftsman and could spend
hours at his work and never get bored. But he would like
to have some company now and then, he said.

I didn't know for sure that I would make it, but now here
I was, for reasons of my own, and he cleared a space on
his table and produced two glasses and I poured my wine,
of which I had more than half the forty ounce bottle left.

"I have started to keep a journal. A combat log you might
call it," said Bernard. We had talked a while, exchanging
information; I learned that for the most part he kept to his
room, going out occasionally to buy books and groceries
and work material. There was a tiny cubbyhole kitchen in
his room and he cooked his own meals.

He handed me a thick wirebound notebook. The hand-
writing was neat, each letter clearly legible, not like my
own scrawl which I sometimes can't read myself.

"There's only one entry," he said. "I started just this morning.' He watched me with his faint and mysterious smile while I read. The date, I believe, was May 12.

I am a General without an army, it began. *There are two kinds of law, the law of the State and the law I follow. These two laws are in contradiction. The law of the State was made in another time and isn't suited to the present age. My law has developed only recently. It is the superior code. I am forced out of conscience to follow it, but it means I must be wary, because in following my law I am breaking the law of the State. Thus when I sabotage a highway, wreck an automobile or a snowmobile, shoot down a helicopter, bomb an oil company, drive a pulp mill out of business, kidnap a politician, I am doing it in obedience to my own code of ethics and for the good of the earth and all its inhabitants. But should I get caught I will be found guilty by the State because I have contravened its statutes of behaviour. They will accuse me of committing a crime against property or against persons. But I repeat, the State's system of legality is outmoded and serves as a hindrance to the welfare of the earth and its inhabitants rather than a help.*

Most people are slow to change their behaviour. You can change their ideas easier but even ideas are very stubborn, the old ideas dig in and give stubborn resistance to the new. Unfortunately there is not time to waste in propagandizing, or should I say proselytizing. By the time sufficient numbers of the public wake up it will be too late. The extent of their unwitting or uncaring destruction will have reached too far, beyond the point of return. There will be a dying giant and nobody around to cure him. He will be too sick to cure himself and barring the unlikely intervention of creatures from another planet that will be the end.

Not everybody is a fool. I am not a fool. I have made my decision to form a guerilla army and fight the machines. Up to now I have been a lone force.

I don't delude myself into thinking I am keeping this record for posterity. The chance of there being a posterity is too remote.

But if I am a casualty before the war is over then it may serve
as instruction to others. I will record mistakes as well as correct
moves, losses as well as victories. In the event my army is
successful—with the aid of similar allied forces which must spring
up if we are to win—then this record will serve as a lesson for
posterity, and a guide for a better morality than I inherited.

"One man isn't enough," Bernard said, when I was
finished reading. "One man is good but say you want to
blow up a factory, something of that size? What's needed
is a commando group."

Although he rarely drank much himself Bernard had bought
a large case of beer in the event of having a visitor, so
when the wine was finished our drinking wasn't.

Later we had a lunch of some soup and cheese.

I was thinking, most people reading what Bernard had
written in his notebook would consider him a crackpot, a
certifiable case. I would have thought that a while back
too. Perhaps, in his extremeness, there was an element to
him that could be described as fanatical and to some
authorities fanaticism is a sickness of the mind. But these
are only judgments some people make about others. To my
way of thinking, and more so to Bernard's, the condition of
the earth was extreme and had been brought on by fanatical
human greed and stupidity. An extreme condition generally
needs an extreme cure. You don't treat a diseased appendix
with an aspirin, you attack it with a knife, you cut it out,
you destroy it. If there were no disease then to cut a man
open with a knife would appear fanatical. It depends on
how you look at things

Bernard drank three or four beers of the two dozen in the
case, and around midnight he became sleepy. Aside from
the effect of this unaccustomed drinking he was in the
habit of going to bed quite early.

But I wasn't tired. I always stayed up late at night and

drinking was nothing new to me. In fact I had, and still
have, an unmistakable partiality to it. Sometimes, however,
particularly when talking to someone, I tend to overdo it.
This was one of those times. I don't know how many beers
I had, I know I had most of the forty ounces of wine. I had
over a dozen pints, and shortly after Bernard went to sleep
I reeled out into the street looking for something to do, for
I felt the night was still in its youth. My memory gets a
little vague around this point. I have elusive visions of
various bars. I know I must have returned to Bernard's at
one point, because where else could I have gotten the sugar?

THE CRIME

It wasn't even a particularly dark street, there were streetlights and store windows with their night lights on, and
several cars drove by, and there were people passing on the
sidewalk. Some of them stopped to watch me. I was holding
the bag of sugar and laughing out loud, a kind of hysterical
chuckling, I kept thinking what I'd tell Bernard in the morning. The people and the moving cars were like shadows in
the dark, spirit things, I paid them no attention at all.
Tottering, stumbling to regain my balance, I found the cap
to the gas tank of a car, fumbled it off, tipped the bag of
sugar. It was a messy job, the sugar poured everywhere. I
thought I must have enough in there. It struck me that I
didn't know how much sugar you had to use. But that must
be plenty, I thought. I tried to put the cap back on but it
wouldn't go, I couldn't find the threads. I tossed it away,
then moved to the next car. I don't recall how many cars I
serviced, probably only two or three because of my drunken
awkwardness. They may have told me later, if they ever
found out exactly, but I wasn't in very good condition for
listening. There were policemen standing beside me. I was

driving in a police car to the station.

"Occupation?"

"Poet." I thought that was a clever thing to say. The cop at the desk wrote it down.

They asked me many questions. I must not mention Bernard, my brain was saying to itself. Although I remember very little it doesn't mean I was unable to think and to retain some cunning and responsibility at the same time. My mind is now virtually blank about that night, but it was not blank then.

If I had no place to stay where did I intend to sleep, they wanted to know. I was seated by a desk and there were detectives facing me.

I was going to spend the night at the train station and then leave for Montreal in the morning, I said.

Where did I get the sugar?

I bought it in a supermarket.

Why was I putting it in gas tanks?

I was going to siphon the gas out and in case I swallowed some I preferred it with sugar.

I don't know if it was that answer or others I made like it, but suddenly a great meaty hand whapped me across the face. My head rang. One of the detectives was swearing at me. They threw me in a cell and I went to sleep.

Sometime in the morning I awoke. I saw the bars when I opened my eyes and I tried to orient myself, to remember what happened. I had a terrible pounding headache, I lay there in a heap of nausea. Then it came to me, vague and sickening memories of cars and sugar and lights and policemen.

"Do you know what you're here for?" said a voice through

the bars.

"I've got an idea what for," I said, sitting on the hard bunk, head in hands.

THE TRIAL

"This is a most unusual case. You are charged with the deliberate destruction of private property, wanton destruction it would appear . . ." The Magistrate had an intelligent and it seemed to me even a kind face. He looked like the fatherly, compassionate, wise sort of man you would ideally assign the god-like position of Magistrate, arbiter among men in matters of life and death, freedom and captivity— those most important conditions of the human body and spirit. He was about sixty with graying hair. His face was calm and thoughtful, eyes alive, curious, probing.

You run across reports in the newspapers of judges who are filled with hate, who pass sentence by the measuring rod of their prejudices, whether they involve youth, politics, race, religion, costume, sex, social status, comportment. Judges as a rule are dangerous men and it's a bad thing indeed to run afoul of them. For instance, if someone were to insult you to your face, call you a moron or a lackey or a hypocrite, and this person is younger and stronger than you, and say his accusations are true—Naturally you don't want to be called these things, even if they are true, but what can you do? With most of us, we can burn up inside and conjure in our minds horrible fantasies of vengeance. But if you're a judge on the bench you can say, "Six months in jail for saying that."

But there's a flaw in the magistrate's power. Almost certainly he has never been a prisoner in jail, thus he's not fully able to savour what he's doing to a man when he sends him there. If he understood what six months in jail was like,

well, it would be just as satisfying sentencing a man to six
days—knowing what it's like—as six months or six years
when you don't have a proper appreciation of what you're
doing.

It's like the difference between playing poker with real
money or with match sticks.

Judges, as some observers have suggested, should for
their own benefit undergo a week in prison before taking to
the bench. It has been done in the past by a few extraordin-
ary jurists, and can be accomplished quite easily using an
assumed run-of-the-mill offence like car theft or embezzle-
ment.

I sensed my judge was not typical when he said "it would
appear" that I had wantonly destroyed the automobiles, or
attempted to. He was curious about me.

I stood just inside the door of a large room. It was more
like a private study than a courtroom. The Magistrate sat
behind an enormous elevated desk in the furthest corner of
the room. Along the dark panelled walls were bookshelves
with glass doors. There were several padded-leather
chairs. The ceiling was high, the floor was shiny with
polished gray tiles. There were three tall windows with
heavy drapes on them.

My companion, my guard, whatever he was, a small man
wearing glasses who had escorted me from the cell, stood a
little behind me. With the Magistrate were two young
lawyers, one casually half-sitting against the desk, arms
folded, the other standing with hands in his pockets. Like
the Magistrate they eyed me with interest, showing no signs
of animosity. They wore well-fitting suits and vests, jackets
casually unbuttoned. I might remark that I myself was
bearded and wearing denim pants, cowboy boots and an old
sweatshirt with a KILL CARS button pinned on my chest. I
had thought of removing the button, which by the way was
one of Bernard's creations, since it kind of gave me away,

but decided there was no point doing so since the cops
would have already noted it in their report.

After the Magistrate read the formal charge against me, he
said:

"How do you plead, guilty or not guilty?"

"What happens if I plead not guilty?" I said, my voice
sounding the way I felt, anaemic.

"You can have your trial postponed and in the meantime
get yourself a lawyer."

"I don't have money to pay a lawyer," I said. More than
that, the thought of waiting in anxiety for a future trial did
not sit well with me. I wanted to have done with this. I
thought I would be found guilty in an case, having been
caught redhanded with at least twenty witness on the scene.

The Magistrate waited.

"I guess I'll have to plead guilty," I said, "but I'm not
guilty."

"You're not? Weren't you caught putting sugar in the gas
tanks of cars?"

"Well . . . I suppose I was. But you're asking me if I'm
guilty of a crime and you're prepared to sentence me to
punishment. But the owners of those cars and the men who
made them and everyone who profited off them, the dealers,
the insurance companies, the garage owners, they're guilty
of a crime against the natural earth and everything that lives
on the earth. I'm not the guilty person. Why should I be
punished?" I had a hard time getting this out, I stumbled a
bit and stuttered over a few words and did not sound force-
ful because I was physically incapable of any kind of
force, being on the verge of collapsing. The combination of
a severe hangover and my unhappy predicament had squeezed
most of the stamina out of me. However my mind felt sharp
enough. And somewhat to my surprise I wasn't intimidated,
I wasn't overwhelmed by the Magistrate and his courtroom.
It may have been the alcohol still in my blood; it may have

been a courage born out of pure misery.

The Judge and the lawyers whispered together. They were far enough away in that big room that I couldn't hear anything they said.

"Do you think that's the way to cure a problem—and we all realize there's a problem with the automobile and pollution—by taking the law into your own hands?"

"Well . . ." I was reluctant to say yes. There was a limit to how far I could go. I am not made in a heroic mold. Something cunning in me spoke in my ear, saying: "If he thinks you're repentant he'll become sympathetic and might let you off."

"Laws are being enacted to fight pollution," the Judge said. "I will tell you something of my own experience. I have a house in the country and last winter I had a lot of trouble with snowmobiles. I don't have to tell you about those machines, the noise they make, the many cases of trespassing and destruction of property, the mess their drivers leave behind. Now I became very angry about them. But I didn't go and break the law and destroy them myself. I worked with the law, not against it. I brought several offenders to court and had them charged with trespassing and disturbing the peace. They were fined and taught a lesson."

If I had not been in the situation I was in, I would have loved to ask the Magistrate how much they were fined, if they still owned and operated their vehicles (away from his property, of course), if they realized what a real problem they were, if it encouraged other owners of such machines to give them up . . . Many things I could have asked. I could have mentioned that a Minister of the Quebec Government, the Transport Minister who was responsible for the regulating of all vehicles including snowmobiles, himself owned four of them, one for each member of his family. And the Federal Government subsidized companies that made the machines, to the tune of several million dollars each year.

But I didn't say any of this, because the last thing I
wanted was an argument. What I did want was a suspended
sentence. Or a small fine. Or one day in jail. I wanted to
get the hell out of there and on the streets and far away.

"I think that's a very good thing you did," I said, "and if
more people reacted the same way perhaps something could
be done about environment problems. But too many don't
care. And I was very drunk last night. I was visiting the
city and got carried away and got so drunk I can hardly
remember what happened and when I heard cars screeching
by and honking horns and leaving blue smoke behind them
something must have happened to me. That's the only way I
can explain it. So you see, in one way I'm guilty, but I'm
not really, because I was drunk and not in control of myself,
and on top of that I was doing something which the Government should be doing. I was trying to improve our environment."

The Magistrate and the two young lawyers whispered some
more.

Then the Magistrate looked at me for a while. He said
finally: "It's obvious you're an intelligent young man, and I
don't believe that at heart you're a criminal. But there is a
law, and without this law none of us would have any degree
of security. For example, a certain man might decide he
needs those boots you're wearing more than you do because
his feet are sore and he has five children to support. If there
were no law, if he followed his own law, he would be just-
ified in his own eyes in taking those boots from you even if
it meant injuring or even killing you to get them." He waited
a moment for that to sink in. It didn't convince me in the
least, but I nodded my head.

"You understand?"

"I can see what you mean." But it's not the same thing,
I said to myself. Because I don't even step on ants with my

boots, they don't hurt anyone.

"How do you plead?" he said.

"Well, I guess I plead guilty," I said.

"You don't have to plead guilty, as I've told you."

I shrugged, and didn't say anything else.

"I'll have to sentence you, then," he said, "since that's your plea. The best I can do for you is give you a short time in jail. The people who own those cars will naturally be very angry. I can't let you off entirely. I sentence you to ten days in jail. They'll feed you well there and you won't have to worry about a place to sleep for a few days." I had told the police earlier when they questioned me that I had no job in Montreal, that I stayed with different friends; I was a poet, I said, and it was tough making ends meet. I made a point of mentioning that I had a Bachelor of Arts degree though I could make no use of it insofar as employment went. I think my education, common as it is today, didn't hurt me with the Magistrate. It enabled him to accept me as an idealist and not as a common vandal. I was told later by others that had I gotten a different sort of judge, and most of them were different, I would have been lucky to escape with six months. To many persons an automobile is still a sacred thing.

As for going to jail, I told myself, however unconvincingly, that it would be a valuable experience, something worth having in my past.

LED OFF TO GAOL

I was taken to a room in the basement of the police station where a smiling man with thinning blonde hair photographed me front and side, a number beneath my mug—like a genuine criminal. Then I was told to stand on a scale and weigh myself, then my height was measured, and finally, holding

my hand the way you teach a child to write, the blonde man
rolled each of my fingers separately on an ink pad, then
rolled it again on my identification form, thus fingerprinting
me.

After that I was kept in a cell until a guard came for me
and I was taken to a room where there were other prisoners,
newly sentenced, still wearing their civilian clothes. We
were handcuffed together in pairs and loaded onto a van and
driven through the streets of Quebec to the *Prison de
Quebec* on the Plains of Abraham. There were seven other
prisoners besides myself, all men in their twenties, all
French, and they seemed to be in high spirits as though this
was an old and not unpleasant routine to them. They laughed
and joked with each other and when we passed a pretty girl
on the street they waved and shouted at her through the
barred window of the van. I was not able to put up such a
front, the best I could do was grin weakly.

The van pulled up at the door of an old graystone building
with bars in the windows. We were herded inside, our hand-
cuffs were removed, then we were led straight to a mess
hall for a bite to eat. It was a large room with three long
rows of picnic-style tables with benches attached. We lined
up at a small window giving onto the kitchen and were
handed each a tray of food. This particular tray held soup,
bread, sausages, a scoop of potatoes and green beans, not
bad if you were in any way hungry. When we were seated an
inmate came around with a huge pail of coffee and ladled
it into enamel cups. Our only eating utensil was a table-
spoon, it was like this at all meals, I soon learned, so you
had to butter your bread with the spoon as well as cut your
meat and stir your coffee. I ate a little bread and soup and
drank some coffee but I was far from having an appetite.

After the meal we were ushered away to be processed into
the prison. I was told to hand over whatever I had in my
pockets. As usual, as happened at every turn I took, and as

was to be expected, I was spoken to in French and had to mumble, "Sorry I don't understand French." I was half afraid I'd be cursed at as a "maudit Anglais!" and kicked in the head but it never happened. Instead they spoke to me in English and with no animosity that I could see.

My valuables consisted of a wallet with twelve dollars in it, a bit of change, the keys to my little apartment, and a slightly used handkerchief. These items were placed in an envelope and I signed a paper which listed them.

While counting my money, the officer said, "How come you put sugar in those gas tanks?"

"I was drunk," I said.

He shook his head, mystified.

In another room I had to strip and take a shower. Then I was given my jail costume of a baggy pair of gray cotton pants with no front pockets, a shirt of the same colour and material, a pair of undershorts and an undershirt, gray woolen socks and old black army boots. They also gave me a towel which every inmate carried around with him, in most cases folded up in a little ball in his back pocket. Once dressed I was taken through a series of barred doors which were locked behind me and at the end of the journey deposited in a large ground-level room with a crowd of other men. A heavy metal door with a small barred peephole in it slammed shut behind me.

I found myself in the midst of a wrestling match. A number of heads turned to look me over and there were some shouted comments and hoots of laughter thrown my way, probably because of my beard. Not understanding a word I replied with my sickly grin and sidled along the wall and leaned against it, trying my best to become invisible.

There was a lot of hollering and thrashing about as the two wrestlers, one a boy around eighteen with the build of a bulldog, and the other a middle-aged man with a great paunch on him, rolled and flopped around on the cement floor. There was no end of grunting and groaning and punching and stomping, in the burlesque style of professional wrestling, and there was only a little seriousness in it all, enough to frighten me.

I decided to have a look around. I hadn't lost all my shakiness but my headache had left me and thankfully I didn't feel I was going to throw up anymore.

There wasn't much to look at. Besides the room I was in there were two others of similar size connecting with it by open doorways. Along the walls were benches. In one room there were three rough picnic tables. Through barred windows you looked out on the prison yard and stone walls which must have been fifty feet high. There was nothing in the yard but a paved surface. There was nothing in the common rooms but a few benches. It was a very simple prison. I soon found out there was nothing much to do here but wait. There were two segregated wings, the one I was in where sentences ranged up to six months, and a wing for those doing longer stretches. I later saw the long-termers out the window. On days when an outdoor exercise period was permitted they did their pacing or sitting in the yard at a different time from ours.

There were two toilets in the common rooms. They stood on a slightly elevated part of the floor in compartments with no doors, and the bowls had no seats. When I strolled by a man was sitting there with his pants down around his ankles having a crap. You either had to shit in public or keep it to yourself.

My stroll didn't last long because it took but a minute to see what was to be seen. There were some two hundred men in the three rooms, some sitting on the benches, some pacing slowly and methodically, several standing talking together. At the moment a few dozen were watching the wrestling match near the entrance. I discovered before long that of these two hundred men I was the only English-

speaking one among them, although some of them were
able to speak one form of English or another along with
their native French.

I noticed someone was talking to me, though for a moment
I wasn't sure he meant me. It was the paunchy man that I'd
seen wrestling. He handed me a crumpled package about a
third filled with tobacco. Stuck in with the tobacco were
some papers.

"For me? Thanks. *Merci*," I said. I couldn't understand
why he was giving me tobacco. I had quit smoking cigarets
about a year before but I had a suspicion I was going to
start again with a lot of time on my hands, so I accepted
the tobacco. Was it because I looked so lost, I wondered?
Later I found out it was the custom, tradition or whatever
to give each newcomer a bit of tobacco as a welcoming
gesture. The fat man, I learned, was the trusty, and it was
to him you went when you needed toilet paper. He handed
out little rolls with no cardboard cylinder in the middle,
they were fashioned by him, probably four or five out of a
regular roll of paper. You carried your toilet paper in one
back pocket and your towel in the other.

At five o'clock we had supper. The food wasn't bad, better
than you'd expect considering the dismalness of the rest
of the place. But I still wasn't hungry, I ate only a few
spoonfuls.

At six o'clock we were marched two-by-two to our cells.
I was grateful for that because I'd been feeling nervous
and uncomfortable. I was anxious to get by myself. The
lone English-speaking person among two hundred French
Canadians, still trembling inside from the drunkeness of
the previous night and the experiences since morning, not
knowing what was coming next—under the circumstances
the privacy of a cell was welcome.

I was taken to a cell block two levels high and placed in
a line at the bottom level before one of the narrow barred

doors. A sergeant with a thick ginger moustache came along with two guards, and holding a clipboard before him checked off our names. Then we disappeared into our respective cells and a guard passed along the corridor slamming the heavy metal locks shut. Other guards were performing the same duty in other corridors and the sounds clanked and echoed off the walls.

It was still bright out and across from my door was a tall barred window. We were in an upper part of the building and through the window I was able to see over the great wall outside and across the Saint Lawrence River where the hills and trees and tiny houses and a silver roofed church looked very peaceful. It seemed very far from where I was, a pointedly different sort of world. Despite telling myself I was only to be here ten days I felt lonely and hopeless as hell.

Once you stepped into your cell you were on a bed. The space was so small that the bed touched the walls on both sides and at the far end, and at the cell entrance there was a space of one foot, and most of this was taken up by a bucket-sized tin can which gave off a strong smell of disinfectant. This was the toilet. To give you an idea how narrow my quarters were, when I lay on my back I could put my two forefingers together and touch both walls with my elbows. When it got dark I learned that the only light available was what came through the bars from the dusky corridor. By the prison routine all inmates were locked in their cells from six in the evening until six in the morning.

I hardly have to say I felt very little romance about my situation. As a youngster I imagined that being in jail was somehow a romantic experience, no doubt because of the influence of various novels and movies. Now, with night coming on, that desolate twilight time, other inmates yelling and swearing and singing, a few transistor radios turned up full blast, filthy whitewashed rough stone walls beside

me, I felt like a hapless orphan. I told myself it was a good
thing I wasn't facing a six-month sentence, the despair
would be unbearable. I had a pencil with me, they let me
keep my pencil and a little notebook I carried, and I debated
marking up a "1" on the wall, because I'd almost completed
one day of the ten. But it seemed more logical to put the
mark there the following morning. I had a few matches, I'd
found a card with a couple in it stuck in with the tobacco,
and I rolled a cigaret. Later I rolled another one, then
another one, using up the last match, and after that I chain-
smoked. It wasn't until the next day I learned to split my
paper matches in two, something I should have thought of
myself. Smoking was a faint comfort, though it made me
dizzy after such a long period of abstinence. The evening
dragged on slowly. I had my thoughts, my tobacco, and ten
days to wait. As anyone knows, nothing makes time drag
like waiting.

I realize there are those who would accept my situation
with a shrug, say what the hell, I might as well be here as
in Iceland. But I suspect I am more of a coward and a weak-
ling than many others. Consequently being where I was
depressed me. I'll confess that when I crawled under my
rough woolen blankets I was on the point of tears. I usually
sleep without a pillow, but when I shoved aside the lumpy
pillow on my bed and lay my face on the mattress cover I
was met by a revolting smell of vomit. I retained the pillow
after that.

To help put myself to sleep, to try and find some comfort,
I reverted to an old practise of my younger days; I started
saying the Rosary on my fingers. Was I still a believer? It
didn't really matter. I had no scruples about using my old
friend the Virgin Mary for a night even if I was a heretic or
agnostic or whatever. It *was* comforting, in any case, and
I drifted off to sleep sometime during the third decade of
Hail Mary's. I was able to make it through the subsequent

nights on my own.

I was awakened in the gray of the morning by a guard
opening the cell doors with his big iron key. My sleeping
mind had stayed alert to where I was so waking was not a
shock. The guard had gone past my door and I noticed it was
open a few inches. I put my clothes on and sat on the bed
and waited. Nobody had told me what I was to do. Then I
saw some other inmates going by carrying their pails so I
picked up mine and followed them.

In a washing room with rows of sinks there were two
toilets against the wall and I stood in line at one of these,
because that's what everybody else was doing. I saw they
were dumping their buckets. When it came my turn I dumped
mine, though there was nothing in it but some liquid disinfectant, then rinsed it out in a sink as the men before me
were doing. I thought I would have to keep alert and watch-
ful so that I could learn what I was supposed to do. It didn't
appear anyone was going to instruct me. I splashed some
water on my face and picked up my bucket and followed the
flow of listless men back to the cells.

There was a few minutes of hanging around near the
washroom after that, until we were lined up and paraded
down to breakfast.

As each man finished eating he got up and went to the
common rooms.

I was let in through the steel door and it was locked behind
me.

I spent a day of sitting, pacing, smoking. You could smoke
in the common rooms without wasting matches, because on
one of the walls there was an electrical contraption that
served as a lighter. You pressed a button and it made a
buzzing and sparkling sound and a jagged thread of fire
danced between two circuits. It looked like a miniature

version of something out of a mad scientist's laboratory.

There were men of all ages in the prison, but most of them were old beaten looking guys, derelicts in for drunkeness. At that time in Quebec, I don't know if it's the same now, there was a law that graduated the jail terms for drunkeness convictions. The first time you got a sentence of a week, the second time a month or so, and the third time and every time after that you got six months—unless you could pay a substantial fine, of course. During those six months a man was confined half the time to a tiny cell, and the other half he spent in three connected rooms like three cement boxes with a large number of other men and nothing to do besides pace the floor or sit and stare into space. Some of the men I saw looked like zombies, pacing slowly along the walls, stopping a moment when face to a wall, turning around methodically and retracing their steps passing by each other like slow drifting ghosts.

Those of the inmates who had money could buy tobacco; the others did without or bummed what they could. A lot of the older men had spent a great deal of time in the prison for drunkeness. They would serve their six months, get out, and inevitably be picked up drunk and have to serve another six months.

Some days, if the weather was good, the inmates were permitted to go out in the yard for two hours in the afternoon. But out there, although you had the fresh air, the scene was more of the same: men pacing, men sitting in abstracted silence, some men talking in groups, some of the younger ones exploding their energy by wrestling and fooling around.

Now and then someone would say something to me in French, but I had to give them an apologetic look and say I spoke English. A few of the young guys asked me what I was in for. They were able to speak a little English.

"Stealing a car," I said.

"What did dey give you, 'ow much time?"

"Ten days."

"Ten days!"

"Yeah."

"You were very lucky. It could 'ave been at leas' two month."

"Yeah. I guess I got a good judge."

That day, my first full day there, was the longest I've ever had to put in in my entire young life. I was wearing a watch and I couldn't keep from looking at it every so often, waiting for my sentence to get over with. As short a time as ten days seems, when five minutes takes two hours to go by, ten days is like an awful long time.

Fortunately I was able to buy tobacco and matches. The bit I was given didn't last long. It happened to be the right day for it because supplies were sold only twice a week. I smoked and smoked until my mouth was raw. The hours were divided into innumerable cigarets. If you did nothing at all, if there was no sequence of events, no markers along the way, it was like being trapped in eternity. I shoved minutes behind me with cigarets. The thought of six months of such days, which was the prospect for many of the others, was almost beyond my comprehension.

When six o'clock finally dragged around I was again eager for my cell. So many people surrounding me in the close quarters of the common rooms put my nerves on edge. Having never thought of myself as a convict I felt sorely out of place among the others who were plainly experienced, perhaps even natural prisoners. I was afraid they might find me out for what I was. Should they learn I was a mistake, not a criminal at all, that the clothes I was wearing were a masquerade, there was no telling what might happen. I avoided looking at anyone, I paced as others did, slow and dreamy; I sat on the rough benches with a vacant look on my face (so I imagined). I pretended to be deep in my thoughts and waiting out my time. I tried to be a part of the background. When someone spoke to me it terrified me. I was

fearful of giving myself away. It seemed to me the others
were here because it was their way of life and I was an
outsider who had stumbled by sheer accident in among them.
I felt like a lamb in wolf's clothing.

In my cell I was able to relax somewhat. Time dragged
there just as slowly but my locked door gave me a sense of
safety. I had not had a shit in over two days, and though I'd
felt an impulse to during the day I resisted it rather than sit
on a toilet in plain view of two hundred men. I know this is
an unnecessary inhibition, but I have it and it's very hard
to put aside. Now, in my cell, I thought, if I feel the urge to
shit I have my own little can. But that was not easy either.
For one thing, the cells were close together and with barred
doors not being exactly soundproof you could hear men along
the corridor coughing, burping, farting, blowing noses, even
breathing. When someone was on the can you knew it. That
meant they could hear me too. But, I told myself, they won't
know it's me because they can't see me. Maybe the two guys
on each side of me and the fellow up above would know, but
that's all. And they couldn't be sure. But it still inhibited
me when I was on the can. But worse than that, the guards
often came strolling by and the can was wedged between the
head of the bed and the bars, so you would be only inches
from the guard and in plain view of him if he came by. Moreover it was very cramped and sitting on a tin can is no
pleasure. I was constipated for something like four or five
days. After that I attempted a few craps on the stage downstairs and others, with more success, on my own personal
can.

The following day I discovered there was a library in the
prison, and that the inmates had the privilege of borrowing
two books a week.

"They have English books too," one of the inmates told

me. He had been kind enough to inform me that it was this
afternoon that you could go to the library, the one afternoon
of the week it was open.

I have always been a big reader of books but I never
wanted a book to read as badly as I did then. From the
library, a one-room establishment but quite heavily stocked,
I took out *The Grapes of Wrath* and *The Good Earth*. They
were pocket books and were protected by brown paper covers.
Clutching them like bags of gold I sat at one of the picnic
tables in the south room (the three connecting rooms formed
an L) and flipped through the pages, then looked out the
window facing me at one of the walls, then took a pleasure-
fully long time deciding which book to begin first. There
was no rush about making up my mind, nor was there about
reading when I started. I decided on Steinbeck's first since
I'd meant for some time to read *The Grapes of Wrath*. I read
the first paragraph, then read it again, examining each word
carefully before proceeding to the next paragraph. I was
indeed a grateful man. Not only had I something to read
which would help me put the time in, but it would be obvious
to the other inmates that I was busy reading and not in need
of someone to talk to. There were quite a few other men
with their noses in books, and later on I noticed they traded
amongst themselves, something I couldn't do because I had
the only English books. But I observed too that a good many
of the men didn't bother to get books; the zombies continued
their perpetual slow marches, or their vacant-eyed vigils on
on the benches; the younger fellows were too busy gabbing
or shoving each other around; and probably there were men
who couldn't read.

When I finished two pages I closed the book and got up
and paced around the room for a while, in order to alternate
my activities, all two of them. When I'd done about ten minutes of walking I sat down again and very slowly and
deliberately resumed reading, sometimes going over the same

lines three or four times. There was a perceptible movement
of time. I felt that I had been partially rescued from my
sentence. I believed now I could get through the remaining
days. Before I'd had my doubts, I was afraid I might suddenly start crumbling into little pieces.

Despite my attempts at invisibility—let me say this once
more, perhaps I can get it straight—I was periodically spoken
to in a string of unintelligible French, and it was, as I've
mentioned, embarrassing to interrupt and mumble I couldn't
understand. Whoever was talking to me either left it at that
and walked away, or he stayed to talk with whatever English
he possessed. When that happened I had to play a part and
for me that is very difficult. I had to lie about my crime. I
said I stole a car. I didn't dare tell the truth because I was
quite sure I would not be understood. That's the problem,
you understand, when you're doing someone a favour and
he can't see where it's a favour, in fact it might well look
like an affront, an injury to him. I wouldn't want anyone to
do *me* such a favour, like burn my house down so I could
experience the joy of sleeping under the open sky. Sabotaging
the modern world was a ticklish assignment to give yourself
because it was easy to see where such a moral decision
was open to abuse, where any nut could try and shape the
world his way despite the victims he might leave behind in
doing it. But that's the way it goes. You have to act by
your own lights.

Probably none of the men in with me owned a car. But
probably every one of them would like to. Stealing a car
then was understandable, a realistic thing to do. Destroying
cars had to be the work of a madman.

When we were getting ready to parade up to our cells that
evening one of the men said to me, "Dere's anudder guy
speaks h'English 'ere, 'e got 'ere dis afternoon, 'e wants to

see you. I'll show you 'im tomorrow."

While waiting to go down to breakfast next morning a
slightly-built man with a tanned face and a neat moustache
appeared at my elbow. "Am I glad to see you, I thought I'd
go nuts in here," he said. "I can't make out what these
gazoonies are saying at all, can you?"

His name was Dan Kiley, he said. He was in his mid-
forties and looked a bit like a smaller-sized, down-and-out
version of Clark Gable. Because of him I never got around
to reading *The Good Earth*. I had gotten a start on *The
Grapes of Wrath* and managed to finish that book by reading
in the dim light of my cell, but during the day I was content
enough to listen to Dan tell stories.

For want of a better way of doing this I will give him a
chapter to himself, since I didn't say all that much myself
but mostly listened. The appearance of the days were the
same, sitting on a bench indoors, or on the hard pavement
in the yard leaning back against the wall in the sun, smoking
steadily, Dan talking, me listening. It made the time pass
very well.

DAN TELLS SOME STORIES

Riding the Rails

"I did an unwise thing, that's why I'm here with you
today, my friend. I didn't come here by choice but I deserve
my fate, it's a case of justice being done, and perhaps it
will teach me a lesson though I doubt it. I'm a traveller by
profession but I never go by train, it would make no sense,
only in a moment of foolishness would I take a train. In
my business I have to stop at as many towns as possible
and when I'm on the road I can usually, if you'll pardon the
expression, put the bum on whoever picks me up. But—as

sometimes happens, and it happens as often as possible— I
was in a state of drunkeness yesterday and found myself
beside a railroad track just outside this very city. I don't
know what I was doing there, I think the track happened to
be beside the highway, and as I sat on the grass passing
the time a line of boxcars came slowly by with the doors
open. Whatever possessed me I cannot say, but I climbed
into a car. It went for a few hundred yards and then stopped.
Then it began backing up. Then it started forward again
and stopped once more. This train, I thought, is not going
anywhere, so I commenced to disembark. When my feet
touched ground I felt an apelike hand on my collar. It
belonged to a railroad cop.

"This morning I said to the judge, 'Your Honor, I am
travelling to New Brunswick to work in the woods, and
being in financial distress at present that was the only
train I could afford to ride. I am sure you can sympathize
with a man when he's hard up, the state of the economy in
the country being what it is.'

"He was a miserable looking old bastard. He looked down
his long nose at me and said, 'Two weeks. Next.'

"I admit I'm a little concerned about being in here, you
see there's a warrant out for my arrest in Vancouver. But I
doubt if they will transport me all the way out there. It was
a mere ten dollar cheque and for ten dollars I can't see
them going to the expense of sending me with an escort all
the way to Vancouver. That, also, was a foolish thing for
me to do, cashing that cheque. But men do foolish things
under the influence of drink. It was a particularly bad act
because in my past there is a little matter of two years
where I was a guest at Kingston Penitentiary because of
writing cheques. They would not hesitate to give me the
same or more on a similar charge."

His Beginnings

"My father was a band leader in Windsor, it was a dance band, and for a while I played clarinet with him. Then he died and I got married and next thing I found myself owning a little farm away out in the sticks. That may sound strange when you look at me now, but at the time it seemed the style of life I wanted, the landed gentry sort of thing. When I was a kid I'd spent summers on a farm with my grandparents and that left many happy memories. But after five years of trying to make a living off my own estate I figured I'd worked enough to last me the rest of my life. I said to my wife, goodbye, you can have everything that's here, for what it's worth—and I left. And I've been on the bum ever since. That was twenty years ago. I'm an unrepentant alcoholic and a bum and I wouldn't be anything else. I'm one of the few free men in this country. So I'm in jail now, but this is a resting place, an oasis. I'll be off the booze while I'm here and I'll eat well and leave healthy as a horse. There's one thing about me, unlike other winos, as the public refers to us, and that is I can eat. Most of the others never eat and that's why they come to grief."

The Great Northern Mining Co.

"I figured even if I was a bum there was no point living like one. I got hold of a few dollars and bought some sharp looking clothes. I earned the money. I worked occasionally in those days, I painted, cooked, I was a salesman different times, but never long at anything because it was never long before I'd hit the bottle and then invariably I lost my interest in being employed, particularly since I'd be fired by then for being drunk on the job or not showing up for work. Anyway, as little work as I did I felt it was too much, and

on top of that I felt I was living beneath my station. As an
intelligent man of cultivated tastes I wasn't content living
in Sally Anns with a lot of deadbeats. With my talents I
knew I could do better. And I did. I got hold of a new suit,
got some business cards printed up: John Davidson, Vice-
President, Great Northern Mining Company, Sudbury, Ont.,
very official looking. Then I went travelling the company,
staying at posh hotels, cashing cheques, buying more
expensive clothes and luggage, laying out big tips, drinking
the best booze. That was the life I'd been designed for. I
got more business cards made with different companies and
different pseudonyms so I wouldn't leave too broad a trail
behind me. Of course business cards and expensive clothes
aren't enough to make the full impression, you need the
right mannerisms, the correct attitude. When you walk into
a hotel you've got to look like you own the place. If you
fit the part nobody's going to want to offend you by demanding excessive proof that you are who you say you are.

"Except sometimes I'd run into a desk clerk or a manager
who must have been burned before. I remember once I tried
to pay my bill with a cheque and the clerk balked and
called the manager. The manager said they didn't take
personal cheques unless, and he was very polite about it,
they were perfectly satisfied with the identity of the guest.
My story apparently didn't satisfy him. I gave him a difficult
time about it but I knew by the stubborn look in his eye
that I was going to have some trouble. In fact the more I
talked the more suspicious he became. Finally he said,
'I'm afraid I'm going to have to call the police and have
them check things out. If your story is true, and I'm sure it
is, we'll owe you a great apology. I would like to accept
your cheque and personally I would, but I can't go against
hotel policy.' Well, what could I do? I couldn't pay the bill,
I had only ten dollars in my pocket. And I couldn't run,
because the manager was a giant of a man and the clerk

was there as well, and there were husky bellhops hanging around. I'd never have made it to the door. And besides, that wasn't my style. I said, 'By all means call the police. I'd like nothing better, anything to clear this matter up. I've never been treated in such a deplorable manner before, I assure you,' and so on. I was highly indignant. Pretty soon a detective arrived and I immediately said, 'Good day, sir, I'm glad you got here, my name is Davidson of the Great Northern Mining Company, and I'm having a deuce of a time with this gentleman here.' I immediately took the initiative, I handed him my card and began complaining about the treatment I was getting. 'What kind of fool would carry a couple of hundred dollars around in his pocket?' I said, for I owed the hotel a hundred and eighty. 'What in hell were cheques invented for if you can't use them?' After I'd finished my spiel the detective looked at the manager and said, 'Well?'

"The manager was not a hundred per cent sure of himself, not by any means. Remember, I didn't look like a bum or anything, you could see my luggage was good quality, and I was putting on a good performance of an indignant executive. 'I'm really sorry to cause this trouble,' he said, 'but our hotel has lost money over bad cheques in the past and lately we've been taking no chances. Believe me, it's nothing personal, I quite willingly accept your story but I can't ignore the policy.'

" 'Look,' the detective said, and I could see he tended to believe my line, just by the way he acted, 'we can settle this very easy. It's just a matter of making a quick call to Mr. Davidson's company and verifying his identity.'

" 'Of course, of course,' said the hotel manager. 'It's really no trouble at all to clear this unfortunate business up. Naturally the hotel will pay for the call.' Now, you can imagine how that made me feel. They both turned to me and I thought, well, what can I do, I might as well say, 'Okay, you've got me, I throw in the towel.' But what the hell, experience has taught me that it's always best to hang in there until the final bell, a few more minutes wouldn't hurt, so I decided to bluff through to the bitter end. I had nothing to lose. The company I used on my card was a real company, by the way. A phony one could be checked out by simply looking in a telephone book. I said, 'Very well, if you refuse to take my word for it, if you insist on treating me like some sort of criminal . . By all means call my head office.' The manager, who I noticed was getting more uneasy the longer this went on, said, 'No, no, it's not like that at all, it's merely a standard precaution, I certainly do accept your word, Mr. Davidson.' But he didn't offer to forget about the phone call.

"The manager asked the switchboard to put the call through and the detective took the phone. I was in a sweat, at least internally. On the surface I was careful to keep my composure. For what reason, I'll never really know. My heart was down in my shoes, the show was going to be over any second now. 'What? What's that you say?' the cop was saying into the phone. 'Nobody there? Goddammit. That's right, so it is. I never thought about that.' He hung up. 'Their offices are closed today, it's the Labour Day weekend.' He looked like he thought he'd been made a fool of. 'Oh my, I never thought of that either,' said the manager. Nor did I. It was Monday, but it was just like any Monday to me. Why they never thought of it, I don't know, perhaps because cops and hotel managers work weekends and confuse them with ordinary days. In any event I said, frostily, 'Well?'

The detective seemed somewhat peeved now, and he said, 'Look, this guy seems all right, I don't know what the fuss is about.' By now the manager had had enough, he had been watching me closely as the call was made and my composure evidently satisfied him. He was probably already thinking of the row my company was going to raise when I reported the treatment I'd received at his hands. He suddenly began

pouring out apologies and explaining over again how they'd
been bitten before by bad cheques, and he hoped I wouldn't
hold anything against the hotel. I was careful not to show
my relief, in fact I was more cool and disdainful than ever.
When he stated he would be happy now to accept my cheque
I didn't let it go at that, I said I was in need of a few dollars
cash—'so I don't have to risk arrest everywhere I go'—and
informed him I wished to write a cheque for $250. 'Of course,
of course,' he said. So I not only got my bill paid but I made
seventy dollars cash off the deal.''

He Donates His Luggage

"Once, and this was when events weren't proceeding so
smoothly as they might have—I'd hocked my good luggage,
and my clothes though neat were on the seedy side—I tried
the manager of a small hotel with a cheque and he too said
nothing doing. No amount of persuasion would move him.
Finally I said, 'My good man, rather than be angry, I must
admit I understand your concern, because there are any
amount of crooks and con-men on the loose these days. The
laws are too lax. I'll go this minute to my bank and get a
certified cheque. Or would you prefer cash?' So I left my
luggage with him, walked out and never came back. My suitcase was an imitation leather thing I'd picked up at the Sally
Ann for fifty cents and the only thing in it was a big rock I'd
found in a park and wrapped in newspapers. So for fifty
cents I'd dined, slept and imbibed a quart of scotch a day
for three days, which was a reasonable exchange, I thought.''

A Trip to the Locksmith

"Another time I was at a hotel and I could tell by the way

the manager was eyeing me that he was entertaining certain
suspicions. I'd been there about a week and I was trying to
think of a way to get out. I knew he wasn't going to take a
cheque just because I asked him nicely, and it being an
ordinary Tuesday there was no holiday in sight to save me
this time. He had already hinted a few times that he wanted
a payment on my bill. Now I could have simply walked out
and not come back, but there was one hitch: I was stone
broke and at this juncture in history I possessed two pieces
of luggage, one a cheap worthless suitcase, and the other
a very expensive alligator item left over from my prosperous
days of not so long ago. I was dying for a drink but I didn't
have the nerve to put another bottle on my bill. That would
have been the last straw. The obvious answer waↄ to take
that good suitcase with me, I knew I could get an easy thirty
bucks for it. I'd bought it with my signature for a couple of
hundred at a good luggage shop and it was like new. But
that was a problem, how was I to get my suitcase past the
desk?

"There was nothing in either piece of luggage but rocks
and newspapers, so what I did, I emptied the good one and
removing my jacket and tie and rolling up my sleeves I took
the elevator to the lobby with the alligator suitcase in hand.
It was open, see, but I'd turned the lock so it wouldn't
close, and holding it with both hands I went to the desk and
said to the clerk, 'Where's the nearest locksmith? This damn
thing seems to be broken.' And I gave a little demonstration
of how it wouldn't close. I was very businesslike about it
and he could see I wasn't dressed for leaving, I looked like
I'd been working at my suitcase trying to fix it myself and
finally bursting with impatience and frustration was rush-
ing out to find a locksmith who could do the job right. He
gave me directions and I thanked him and went out the door
and never returned. I quickly merchandized the suitcase,
went to the Sally Ann and picked up another one for a buck

or two, along with a fairly presentable sports jacket and tie, and with the addition of a couple of bottles of wine was on my way."

I asked Dan how he had been finally caught, the time he was sentenced to two years in Kingston.

Because of a Woman

"Because of a woman," he said, "the downfall of many a man. I was shacked up with this thing in Toronto, I don't know where I picked her up but we had a small apartment and were living off some money I'd accumulated in my usual manner. Among the establishments I patronized were jewelry stores. I'd purchase something expensive, off my mythical bank account of course, like a watch or ring or necklace, and then wholesale it to a gentleman I knew who was in the selling business, the buying and selling business. I received only a fraction of the value of the goods but it was a living. Then I made the mistake of getting careless, of becoming overconfident, because I'd been operating for a few years now without being caught. This woman friend of mine, as it happened, had a birthday, and by coincidence I'd recently come into possession of a bit of jewelry which I was about to get rid of promptly as usual. We were at home then, and we were drinking a couple of bottles of scotch, and I said out of the bigness of my heart, 'Well now, since it's your birthday I'll give you a birthday present.' So I produced a lovely pair of diamond earrings worth a few hundred bucks and I said, 'Here you are, my dear.' They were in a velvet-lined leather box with the imprint of the store inside the cover. She was much taken with the gift and I said I'd bought it just for her because, you know, she was not aware of the nature

of my business. She thought I was an honest man with some
money in the bank.

"Well, she gushed over the earrings and said things like,
'They must be *very* expensive,' and like a complete fool I
casually mentioned the price because my ego couldn't resist
making such a fine impression. She was greatly impressed
that the earrings were worth so much, more impressed even
than I thought when I told her. A few days later I came home
to the apartment with a bag of liquor and was greeted by
two cops. My woman friend was there too, crying. I was
arrested on the spot. What she had done, she had gone down
to the jewelry store with the earrings and tried to return
them and get the money. By this time the owner of the store
didn't have a particularly high opinion of the cheque I'd
given him, so he kept her hanging around while he made a
phone call. That's all it took. Two years in the pen because
of a stupid woman."

When he was released Dan tried working at several jobs
but the lure of the bottle was too strong and he was soon on
the road. I mentioned that I had grown up in New Brunswick
and he said, "I've been through there many times. What part
are you from?"

"Chatham."

"Yes, I know Chatham. I spent a week in jail in Newcastle
just up the river. But it was because of being in Chatham."

I asked him what had happened.

A Man of God

"Well, as usual I was looking for a handout, and I saw, you
know, there's this enormous big church at the top of the hill
so I thought I would hit up the priest for a few bucks. The

priest's house was pretty posh looking too, there were a couple of cars in the garage, so I says to myself, 'They are prosperous here and shouldn't mind contributing something to the welfare of the needy,' namely me. I knocked on the door and a young priest answered, he would be an assistant to the parish priest I imagine, and I says, 'Excuse me Father, but I am passing through town and I wonder if you could help me out. I've been looking for work for months now and I hear there's something in Cape Breton but I'm having a hard time getting there. Being a devout servant of God and a Catholic like myself, I'm sure you would not see a poor man forced to sleep in a ditch at night and go hungry in the morning.'

"He looked at me impatiently and in a cold voice said, 'How much do you want?'

" 'Well, Father,' I said, 'I think I could get by with five dollars though I've got a long road ahead.'

" 'Five dollars!' he said. You'd think I asked him for one of his cars. 'Why you must be crazy. I certainly won't give you that.' He said he'd give me a quarter. Twenty-five cents. Well I didn't climb all the way up that hill for twenty-five cents so I began to tell him that if it was during the Depression his offer would be tolerable, but with inflation and rising costs a quarter was only slightly better than nothing. I started into a lecture about Christ, how he had given everything he had to the poor and requested that other Christians do likewise, his disciples in particular, and I said the last place I'd been was the United Church minister in Campbellton and he had given me ten dollars, which didn't happen to be true, he had given me three, but it was better than a quarter. Anyway, this priest, who looked well-fed enough himself, got quite annoyed with me and after a bit of arguing said, 'I'm not listening to any more of this. You're nothing but a bum, trying to live off others. You'd better leave before I call the police.'

" 'Nothing but a bum, am I,' I said. 'You stand there with
your big fucking stomach sticking out while half the kids
in this town are going around starving and you call me a
bum. I'd like to know who's the real parasite between the
two of us.'

"His face turned red as a radish and he started sputtering
and he told me to get going quick or he'd have me thrown
in jail. I laughed at him and turned and walked away. Well,
I wasn't that far down the street, walking along taking my
time, when the cops drove up and stopped. The good father
must have called them soon as I left. To compound matters
I had a bottle of rubby tucked in my belt under my shirt. I
got a week in the county jail in Newcastle and then according
to the script was told to get out of town. Before getting on
the highway I paid a call on the Anglican minister in Chatham,
a nice old guy, and he gave me five bucks and bought me a
bus ticket to Moncton. Some you win and some you don't."

Reuben

"The laws in this country leave something to be desired.
I am normally a wine drinker, but on Sunday in some strange
town where are you going to get a bottle of wine? The liquor
stores are closed and if you find a bootlegger he'll charge
you double. A man in my circumstances can't afford to pay
overly inflated prices. But I need a drink all the same so
what I generally do is go to a drugstore and buy a bottle of
rubbing alcohol. It's not the smoothest drink in the world
but you can get used to it and it serves the purpose. Some
drugstores are all right, they know what you want the stuff
for and they don't argue. But then you get these donkies
who think they know what's best for you, they want to pro-
tect you from yourself, while you're standing there shaking
and ready to fall apart, and they won't sell it to you. So

just to be safe I give them a story, it might be the only drugstore for miles. I walk in limping, for instance, I say I got a terrible pain in my leg, or I tell them I've got arthritis in my shoulder, or I've strained my back. I ask if they've got anything I can rub on the sore spot to ease the pain. Once I hobbled into a place and asked if they had anything for the pain in my leg, I said I heard there was a liniment that was good for a pulled muscle. I was going to grope around and come up with the name of a brand of rubby when the dumb jerk behind the counter says, 'I've got just the thing,' and he rummages around and brings out a bottle of something, I don't know what it was, olive oil or something, and I looked it over and I knew it was not something that I wanted to drink. Meanwhile I've already spotted the reuben on the shelf, and I says, 'Well, uh, I don't know if this would work, how about this stuff here,' and I reach up on the shelf and take down a bottle of rubby. He looks at me, throws the bottle in the bag, says 'sixty-five cents,' and I walk out, only it's kind of embarrassing and in my hurry to leave I forget to limp. As I'm going out the door the guy calls after me, 'It's working already!'

"Another time I was in a town in Ontario where they've got a race track, just a small town, and it was Sunday and I had a vicious thirst on. I was walking down the street and since I'd noticed this track on the way in I stopped a kid and said, 'I see you have some horse racing here.' He says, 'Yeah, that's right.' And I says, 'I used to know a man around here, he's got a couple of horses up at the track, what's his name now . . .' And I look like I'm thinking hard and the kid says, 'Might be Jack Duncan, he owns quite a few,' and I says, 'That's right, kid, Jack Duncan's the name. Think I'll pay a call on him. Thanks.' So I continued down the street till I came to the drugstore and I go in and say to the man at the counter, 'Hello, I'm working for Jack Duncan now at the track and we got a few sore horses. I

gotta pick up some liniment.' 'Oh yes, certainly,' the guy
says, very eager to be of help, 'how much would you like?'
Well, while I was there I thought I might as well make the
most of it, so I says, 'Well, I might as well take a gallon
while I'm at it, so I don't have to keep running down for it
all the time.' I knew they sold it by the gallon in some
stores, though I think they rarely sold it in that quantity
for drinking purposes. It happened that this place had the
gallon bottles, most likely because of the track with all
those horses. I gave the man the money and he gave me a
receipt and I walked out with enough reuben to keep the
fires burning for a little while to come. Actually it was too
much to carry around, but I chanced upon a few more bums
and between us we got to the bottom of the bottle."

The Sally Ann

"Things don't always run smooth, I try my best but I don't
manage to get a hotel room every night. To keep up my
present style of living costs five or six thousand a year
and it requires a good deal of effort to raise that sum. A
bum's life is not all pleasure. I used to stay at the Sally
Ann sometimes but not anymore. To my mind they're hypo-
crites, the Salvation Army. They figure themselves very
holy bastards helping poor sinners and they feel quite
proud of themselves. That's their kick, they force poor bums
and winos to repeat prayers and sing hymns and carry on
like trained monkeys in return for a sandwich and a bowl of
soup, and it makes them feel full of virtue. The guys they
throw handouts to are never let forget what common tramps
they are and the scum of the earth who should be humble
and grateful that a better type of person is stooping to help
them. I remember once we were sitting at this prayer meeting we had to put up with, and there were special guests

there, politicians or some rich contributors to the fund, and
this Major was on the stage doing his best to impress them.
He was there talking to these slummers and he was all
smiles telling them what great work he was doing and how
happy the poor down-and-outers were now they were being
helped. And he says, 'And now we'll have a hymn.' And he
turns from his guests and you know, the change in his face—
when his eyes moved from them to us the expression on his
face suddenly went from angelic to stern and commanding,
and he says to us, 'We will now sing *Onward Christian
Soldiers*' or whatever, and the way he said it and that rotten
look on his face, it was like he said, 'Alright you peasants,
you will now sing this hymn—or you don't eat.' "

When he related this, Dan mimicked the man. He possessed
an excellent mimic talent and he varied the voices for the
different characters in his stories. Though we were sitting
at that time in the sun in the yard, from the expressions on
Dan's face you saw a Major standing in his stiff uniform on
a platform at the Sally Ann, the smiling and ingratiating
Major at one moment, then the ramrod parade square officer
commanding his subordinates the next. "These days if I go
to the Sally Ann I either get a voucher for a hotel room or
I don't take anything," said Dan. "You don't catch me
sleeping in their lousy dormitories. I'd rather sleep in a
zoo."

A Man Who Saw the Light

"There are many crazy individuals in the world, people
who get the feeling they're messiahs, they figure it's their
duty to rescue lost souls, like they got a message direct
from God himself. There was this one guy in Winnipeg who

all of a sudden saw the light. He was a businessman and
he had a bit of money and he got it into his head he was
going to help out the deadbeats around town. He'd have a
prayer meeting once a week and when it was over he'd pass
out money for food. I think it was two bucks for each bum.
Naturally it was a popular gathering, a whole gang of us
would show up and get our two bucks and go out and buy
some bingo. Only the guy soon caught on where his money
was going, and one day he announced: 'Gentlemen, I'm
sorry to say that I'm disappointed in you. I've been given
to understand that you're taking the money I give you for
food and wasting it on liquor. I'm afraid this can't go on.
From now on I will make an arrangement for you to eat at a
restaurant and I will have the bill sent to me.' Well, I was
sitting there with a few of my buddies of the time, and we'd
all sat through that prayer meeting and it looked like we
were going to be deprived of the wine we'd come for. When
the guy finished his speech, which he'd delivered almost
in tears, because he was indeed disappointed in us as he
said, I stood up and in a solemn, heartfelt voice, said:
'Mr. Collins, what you have just said is the truth. It's a
shame but it's the truth. There are men here who have been
taking your money on false pretences and throwing it away
on alcohol. It's disgraceful behaviour and unfortunately
reflects badly on the rest of us who are trying our best to
get back on our feet and resume living decent productive
lives. We are not all drunkards and it would be an injustice
to those of us who are sincere if we are included amongst
those who have deceived you. I know you feel that your
trust in us has been betrayed, but let me assure you that
this is not entirely so. Some have betrayed you, but there
are others who have accepted with gratitude your generosity and walked with heads held high into a restaurant and
purchased much needed food. It was with a sense of dignity
that we ordered and paid for our meal, and for this we are

indebted to you. Now, Mr. Collins, I have a proposal which
I hope you'll agree to. I've been down on my luck for some
time around this city and I know most of the men in this
room. I know which of them are responsible people and
which of them, sadly, are slaves to drink. If you will give
me the money you meant to distribute I will pass it around
to those who won't waste it—and as for the others, for their
own good, you can arrange for them to be fed at a restaurant
as you planned.'

"Well, he was moved by my speech and told me I was an
honest man and an example to the others. 'I can rely on you
to see this is properly distributed,' he said, giving me a
handful of bills. I spread the money amongst my buddies
and we left and promptly got hammered."

The Travelling Salesman

"Some of these travelling salesmen are hard to take, they
pick you up for company and they want to be entertained,
see. I don't mind that because that's part of my business,
I give them a few stories and a few laughs and then hit them
up for a few dollars. But some of those guys are ignorant
sonsabitches, you know the type, loud and arrogant and
stupid. I remember this one fellow, I was making my way
east and I was out around Brandon, and he gave me a lift.
I was just in the car when he said, 'You're on the bum,
eh?' And for quite a few miles I got a gratuitous lecture
about bums on welfare who could be working, and how he
himself had worked his way along and look where he was
now, and he always believed in helping a man when he was
down but he'd only go so far, the man had to help himself,
he couldn't live off society without making his contribution.
So I had to sit there while he gave me this line of bullshit,
you know, he was very hearty about it, and he'd say things

like, 'Now talking man to man' or 'Let's face it, buddy',
horseshit salesman talk, 'I may not have a college education
but I've been through the school of hard knocks.' I just
said yes, yes, you're right, a lot of people should be working who aren't, they're just too lazy. Myself, I said, I
suffered shell shock in the war and have a small pension,
hardly enough to live off. My nerves are very bad but I
travel around trying to pick up some work where I can. But
it's not easy, I'm only able to work for a while, I said,
never for a long stretch of weeks because of my condition.
He reluctantly agreed that I was probably an exception but
he continued flapping his mouth about bums and deadbeats.
He was getting some sort of perverse pleasure out of saying all this to my face, you could tell he was proud as hell
of himself. I don't think he paid much attention to my war
story at all, he was still in his mind telling a tramp what
he thought of tramps. Anyway we drove on for quite a ways
and I was getting a bit hungry, and he says finally, 'Why
don't we stop in at a diner along the way—don't worry, it's
on me.' I couldn't stand the sonuvabitch but I was in the
mood for a bite to eat, so I says okay, it's fine with me.
We pull up at a roadside diner and he takes me in, and there
are people in there sitting at tables, a quiet little place,
and soon as we're in the door, he's got one hand on my
shoulder, he says in this booming voice, 'Give this poor
man a cup of coffee!' Now how about that? 'Give this poor
man a cup of coffee.' Everybody was looking at us. So I
says, in my own booming patronizing horseshit voice, 'One
moment, waiter, I didn't order any coffee.' Then throwing
my last dime on a table I said, 'See this poor bastard gets
a bromoseltzer.' Then I turned and walked out leaving him
with his mouth hanging open.''

His War Record

"Speaking of a war pension, which of course I don't have, the closest I've been to a war was when I was living with my wife, one of my routines is to visit various Legions along the way and tell them my war stories and how hard times have got me now. If I find the right mark I usually do all right. Clothes, food, hotel, money. These guys can get very sentimental about old soldiers down on their luck, I mean as long as you're not a babbling idiot. You have to be able to say the right things and play the right strings."

A Handful of Socks

"You know, when you're a man like myself and you have a strong urge to take a drink you can find yourself doing some shameful things. I try to be a decent person but occasionally I slip and sometimes it can be embarrassing. I recall once, it was in Edmonton, I was strolling around the streets and I walked into a small clothing store. I gave the owner a hardluck story, about how I had a job starting Monday but this was Friday and I had no money for a place to stay till then, and I wondered if he could help me out, give me a small loan which I'd repay out of my first paycheque. Any amount would do, I said. I was asking him out of impulse and desperation, I said, I had never borrowed money before, and so on. Now I was as usual cleanshaven, my hair trimmed and combed, my clothes weren't in tatters or anything, as you'd expect in the case of a wino. I'm very careful about that. As for giving out a good line I might say I am as proficient at this as any bum in the country. So this man, he was not too old, maybe thirty-five, he looks at me a minute, sizing me up, then says, 'I don't normally do this, but—' and at that point a customer came in. Excuse

me, he said, he'd get back to me after waiting on the customer. I said okay, I didn't mind waiting at all. I knew I had
him, he was plainly going to give me a donation. Well, he
was at the back of the store showing the customer some
shirts and I was waiting there, and the next thing I knew I'd
picked up a handful of socks and shoved them under my
jacket. Why I did it I'll never know. It's not like me to pull
a trick like that. But before I could stop myself it was done.
In a minute the fellow came back and handed me a ten dollar
bill. 'I wouldn't give you this if I didn't think you were
sincere, you impress me as an honest man and not just a
panhandler. I've had tough times in the past myself, I know
what it means to get a helping hand when you really need it.
I hope this will assist you.' I felt a bit bad as I walked out of
the store because he had been so generous to me. But I
couldn't very well take the socks out of my jacket and put
them back. I wasn't long out of the store and on my way to
the nearest liquor store when, as fate would have it, a cop
put the grabs on me. He said, 'Where d'you think you're
going? We don't want no bums on the street here. What's that
you got under your jacket?' He was a right mean fucker. He
pulled the socks out and said, 'I saw you coming out of that
store, I thought you were up to something.' He had a hold of
me by the arm so I wouldn't run away, and it was probably a
good idea on his part because if ever I wanted to take my
chances and run that was it. 'Take your hands off me,' I said
indignantly. 'The gentleman in that store was so kind as to
give me these socks.' The cop laughed in my face. 'Yeah,
he gave them to you,' he said. He practically lifted me off
the pavement dragging me back to the store. 'I found this
bum with a bunch of socks on him,' he said to the owner.
'He says you gave them to him.' The cop had a self-satisfied
sneer on his face. The owner of the store looked at me and
it was a sad look indeed. It wasn't an angry look, it was a
look of bitter disappointment and disillusionment. As for

myself I could have easily crawled under the carpet if the cop had left me loose. Never have I felt so low. 'That's right, I gave him the socks,' the owner said. 'You can let him go.' The cop stood there amazed and speechless. Finally it occurred to him to unclamp his hand from my arm. I was as dumbfounded as the cop. I'll be damned if I could think of anything to say, and that is unusual with me, so I just slunk out of the store, ten dollar bill in my pocket and a dozen pair of socks in my hand. I sold the socks to some guy on the street for the price of a wine. This happened six years ago but I'll never forget the disappointed look on that store owner's face. I keep thinking that one day I'll return to his store and repay him his ten bucks and throw in another fifteen for the socks. The only obstacle is I'm not sure I'll ever have twenty-five dollars to spare and be in Edmonton at the same time. But it's something to think about. That man was a real Christian, if ever there was one."

Vegreville

"Most of the time I travel alone, I prefer it that way because otherwise you have to earn too much in the run of a day to pay expenses, but now and again I'll run into one of my old partners and we'll be on the road together for a while. I remember once I was with my buddy Soft Coal and we were going through Alberta. Soft Coal is his nickname, his real name's Jim. I gave him the name because he once told a farmer we did a bit of work for, Jim was smoking some god-awful tobacco and the farmer asked what in hell he had in that pipe, horseshit? Jim says, 'Nope, soft coal.' Anyway we were on the road and hadn't had a drive for a long time, so we were walking along and we came to this little town. As we were strolling into it Soft Coal stopped a young fellow and said, 'Hey kid, where are we, what place is this anyway?'

The young fellow says, 'Vegreville.'

"Soft Coal looks at me then back at the kid. 'Beggarville, eh?' he says. 'Well there's two more beggars in 'er now.' "

Tools of the Trade

"As I was saying, appearance is most important in my line of work. You have to give the impression you're only temporarily on the skids. If you look too far gone the most you're going to pick up are dimes and quarters. You need to maintain a certain air of fallen respectability and look like you're worth saving. A bum who looks like a bum arouses loathing, people draw away from him like he's a leper. But if you look neat and clean and appear to be trying your best to manage through difficult times and if you can interest your victim with a good story then you can come to expect a five or ten buck handout. Now I'm a Christian Scientist, I'm well read in religion, and I've been in many discussions with priests and ministers who are naturally curious about my beliefs and interested in discussing theology. Mind you I don't get disputatious, I don't argue, I discuss. And when they see what an intelligent man I am they feel bound to help me get back on my feet. I always travel light these days, I rarely carry luggage or a pack. It's just too much bother. Occasionally I'll lug a small flight bag along, but I'm in the habit of losing these while drunk. Even if I've got only the clothes on my back I always keep on me a razor, a comb, a needle and thread and some shoe polish. Once I was putting the arm on an old guy with whiskers, he might've been a rabbi, this was in Ottawa, and he was digging out some change— this was another of my lapses, I normally don't stop people on the street, it's an undignified method of cadging and it's not productive. You suffer a lot of discourtesy for small returns. Then again there's the danger of being collared by

the law. But I espied this old character across the street
and it flashed through my mind that he was a rabbi, and a
man of the cloth is my natural prey. I hotfooted it across the
street and gave him a quick story, and without saying anything he was in the process of crossing my palm when the
arm of the law once again descended on my shoulder. And
once again I had a bottle of rubby tucked in my belt. The
cop gave me a frisking and turned up my possessions, the
razor and shoe polish and the rest. He pulled me in and when
I came before the judge the cop was there and in a voice
quivering with righteousness and incredulity, he said: 'Your
Honor, this man is a *professional bum!*' It was like a revel-
ation to him. The description, I might say, was quite
accurate. I remember another judge I appeared before. I'd
been nabbed in the street this time also. As I stood there in
the court the judge announced in a most solemn voice that
I was being charged with, if you can believe it, 'soliciting
alms.' That was a new one for me. I felt like saying, 'Allah
be praised, your Honor!' "

Well, Dan's stories went on and on, and I've only given a
sampler. I told him he should write down the story of his
life. He might have a best seller.

The Literary Life

"Oh, I've thought about being a writer and in fact I did
write a book once. It was about my travels, all the places
I've been. There's not a man in this country who knows
Canada as well as myself. I've been over every inch of it
and more than once. I've been in just about every jail too.
I wrote this book, or most of it, while I was in Toronto. I'd
done some work housepainting, it was one of the times when

I decided to quit travelling and get off the bottle for a
change, sometimes you get the feeling when you're on the
road that it's all very futile, you'd like to stop and get
yourself together for a while. Also you can absorb your fill
of vile little county jails. So I got a job and a nice bachelor
apartment and saved my money. In the evenings I worked on
my book. But this period didn't last, as you may have gathered, and I was back again on the bottle and the road. I took
my book with me and kept working on it when I had a free
moment. I'd do a bit of writing when I got a hotel room, lying
on the bed with a quart of wine and a pencil and paper. Or
I'd stop on the roadside and sit in the shade and scribble
down a few things that had happened during the day or the
past few days or something I remembered. After a while I
felt I'd more or less finished the book and I kept the thing
in a flight bag and carried it around with me. I didn't know
how to go about getting it published but I thought that when
I got back Toronto way I'd look up a good friend there who
writes for the *Globe and Mail* and have him see about it. In
the meantime I was in B.C. and I had an itch to go up to the
Yukon. I'd never been there though I've been up again a few
times since. I'm a profound admirer of Robert Service and I
was curious to see the country he'd lived in. Well, my book
was in the flight bag along with some old clothes I'd picked
up and it was a couple of months since I'd finished it and
I more or less forgot about it. I was sitting on the side of
the road outside Whitehorse sucking on a bottle of wine and
this old squaw came hobbling along looking like she hadn't
had a meal in weeks. She asked me for a few cents so she
could buy a bite to eat. I felt sorry for her but unfortunately
I was broke. I'd scrounged enough for the bottle but not a
cent more. So I says, without thinking, 'Here, take this bag,
you might be able to sell it. There's some old clothes in
there which somebody might buy off you as well.' She
thanked me and went tottering off and I resumed my idle

drinking. I didn't think twice about giving the bag away, it was only a burden to be carrying around anyway. If I wanted another one I could always find one easily enough. So I was sitting there with nothing much on my mind when it suddenly struck me what I had done. I'd given my book away. I jumped up and took off after the squaw but I never found her. She'd gone into Whitehorse and vanished. And that was the end of my literary masterpiece. You might wonder how I could do such a stupid trick. I wonder too. I would have to blame it on the drink which apparently took some alertness out of my mind."

THE END OF THE SENTENCE

Early in the day I had a visitor. The guard called my name about ten times before I realized it was me he was calling. The guards were always shouting out for one person or another and not expecting to be paged myself I got used to ignoring them. It was "L'Anglais" that was wanted, someone said, and someone else came over and said to me, "You 'ave a visitor." A visitor? Me? How could that be, I wondered. Nobody even knew I was here.

I was shown into a narrow room with a long table divided down the center by a screen. There was a bench at the table. On the other side of the screen was Bernard. He was smiling secretly. I sat down opposite him and said, "Hi."

"Hi." Then he started laughing quietly. "How's everything?"

"Good. How'd you know I was here?"

"I heard it on the radio. A Montreal poet." He chuckled to himself some more. "That was something. I didn't know you'd do it. It's a good sign. I've been thinking about it quite

a bit, and I think it's a good sign. It's too bad you got
caught."

"Yeah, well, it's not so bad. It's material for my memoirs.
I've met a very interesting man here, listening to him helps
pass the time away. In fact by sitting here now I guarantee
you I'm missing a good story, because that's what he's doing
down there, telling one of his stories."

"I won't stay long. Do you want me to go now?"

"Oh no. I didn't mean that. How long do they give you to
visit?"

"Half an hour."

"Aren't you kind of, how shall I say it, crazy, I mean
coming here? It strikes me as a foolhardy thing to do."

"Oh?"

"It's a wonder you're not on this side of the screen with
me right now."

He continued smiling. "I knew you hadn't told them about
me. If you had they'd have been around to pay me a call
before the radio broadcast. My first impulse was to change
addresses immediately, but I thought: 'It's unlikely they'll
torture him for information. And if he hasn't said anything by
now I doubt if he'll change his mind and volunteer my name
and address.' So I stayed where I was. I am, I have to tell
you, impressed by what you did." He paused, then said,
"You don't suppose this room is bugged, do you?"

"I doubt it. That would be a rotten thing to do. I don't
think they care about anything here, it's just a place to keep
men off the streets for a while."

"That's what I thought."

"What did you tell them, did they ask a lot of questions?"

"No. I just gave them another name, and I'd brought along
a few papers of my own creation with that name on it. It was
easy. They just said go ahead. They were quite friendly."

Bernard's moustache was growing well, it was long and
bushy.

"I brought you a book," he said.

"Yeah? What is it?"

He slid it through a slot at the base of the screen. It was an anthology of poems, *New American and Canadian Poems*.

"Poems," I said. I felt like sliding it right back.

"You like poems, don't you?"

"I sure do. But . . . I don't get much of a chance to read in here. And I've already got a couple of books from the library."

"Oh. I thought you might like a book. I didn't know you had a library."

"Well, thanks, it was good of you. I appreciate it. I'll read it in my cell."

A book of poems in a prison. It made me shudder. What if the other inmates *saw* it? They would have me then. My convict's cover would be blown, I'd be unmasked for sure. My fellow inmates, they would think I was a queer, or weak and fragile, vulnerable. Anything but a legitimate con. A skin book yes, a comic book, a detective novel even. The main trouble was the low and unmanly reputation poetry enjoys, for some reason.

Nevertheless I kept the book, because it was thoughtful of Bernard to bring it. And he told me he had signed it in and couldn't take it back. Or it would be difficult to, rather strange to explain, and he didn't want to get involved in any situation that attracted attention. So I shoved the book under my shirt and hoped nobody would notice it.

"When do you get out?" Bernard said. I told him it would be a little earlier than expected, or was supposed to be—I wouldn't believe in my release until my feet hit the sidewalk. But from what I'd heard you got a day off for every week there.

"Give me a call," he said.

"You think I should see you? I think I'll just hightail it back to Montreal."

"That's what I was going to suggest. You never know. They might have connected you with me, or with someone. There are others around who are sweetening up cars. They'd have to think about that. They might watch you. That's why I said to phone. You could use a pay phone."

"Okay," I said. Bernard left and I was taken back to the common rooms. The next day my name was called again. This time I caught it.

"Someone wants to see you," I was told by the guard. Another visitor? I asked who and he said he didn't know.

I was escorted to an office. Sitting behind a desk was a sergeant. With him in the room were two young men.

"Have a seat," I was told. My two visitors didn't speak English and so the sergeant acted as a go-between and where necessary a direct translator. One of these gentlemen, I was informed, was the owner of one of the cars that I had operated on. His engine was ruined, he claimed. He was prepared to sue me unless I could settle with him now. His insurance didn't cover sugar in his gas tank. To save us both trouble he would prefer to settle the matter out of court. He wanted fifteen hundred dollars.

"Fifteen hundred dollars!" I said. "Tell him he must be crazy. I've never had fifteen hundred dollars in my life or anything near it."

"You don't have a job?" said the sergeant.

"No."

"How do you live?"

"I do a little freelance journalism." This was true, I had a connection at one of the numerous sex-and-gore tabloids in Montreal and wrote the occasional piece for them. Yes, I did a little freelance journalism, as well as retail the odd lump of hash. I didn't say that last of course. I'm not that stupid. Besides I didn't handle much. Mostly I never had much money. I'm an artist, not a capitalist.

The sergeant talked to the guy in French a while. The car

owner was very animated. He kept giving me peculiar looks
while he talked. His friend was impassive.

"He says you'll have to pay him," said the sergeant, "or
he'll take you to court."

"Tell him to go ahead. I can't give him what I don't have."

There was more French conversation. Again I was told I'd
have to pay. Only this time the bill was lowered to an even
thousand. But it was all the same to me. I repeated that I
had no money and I was unemployed. I said to tell the guy
I was sorry I inconvenienced him, that it was nothing
personal. When that was translated to him he started ranting.
I didn't know what he was saying but it wasn't hard to
imagine: "Nothing personal! What do I care about personal!
My car is ruined and it cost me a lot of money. Does he
know how hard it was to get that car, how I had to work and
save and meet payments? Does he realize how I need it, I
need a car to get to work, and how am I supposed to take
my girlfriend out? Is he crazy or something, he doesn't even
know me. Why did he pick my car? He should be locked up
in a lunatic asylum. I want my money! Tell him he has to
give me the money! Etc."

The sergeant finally concluded we were getting nowhere
and said, "He's definitely going to take you to court and
you'll have the burden of that debt on you for a long time,
because he says he'll sue you for five thousand. And then
you'll have to pay the court costs as well. Couldn't you
borrow the money?"

"Not a chance. My friends are all poor too. So is my
family."

"Well, why not get a job and pay him in installments.
Surely you could get a job, you're young and you've got
an education."

"I don't have time for a job. I'm a poet. That's my job."

"Well, there's nothing I can do. You can expect to receive
a court summons too. Where will you be?"

"I don't know. In Montreal."

I was taken downstairs again, leaving a very angry ex-car owner. I wondered why he had driven his car if there was sugar in the tank. The police must have been careless about informing the owners. Or perhaps they hadn't been able to discover all the cars I'd doctored and warn the drivers. It was my understanding that the car had to be driven in order for the engine to be destroyed. But I don't know much about these things.

I had two more visits of the same nature shortly after and and might have had more—however many cars I serviced that night, or were serviced by other sugarmen or personal enemies of the victims—but no doubt the sergeant convinced the others of the hopelessness of dealing with me. I was already facing three lawsuits and if I ever paid them off I'd be too old to take care of any further suits. But then maybe other litigation was underway anyway without the plaintiffs coming to see me, knowing they could not hope to make a deal out of court.

I thought the car owners were all asking too much money. But it didn't surprise me, for humans are a greedy lot. One of my visitors was a woman. She was fat and did a lot of gesticulating and swearing at me. The other appeared to be a businessman. He spoke to me in English trying to make me realize the seriousness of what I'd done, and how it was my moral and legal obligation to reimburse him for the damage I'd done him. I didn't say much, but I said this much: "I didn't damage you, it was your car I damaged." That had no favourable effect. His car was part of him.

In the morning and evening when it was washup time I observed I was the only man there who brushed his teeth. The reason for this was simple: I was the only man who had a toothbrush. I didn't bring it with me, because like

many of the inmates my happening to be in jail was a matter
of pure circumstance; I had not planned it and so didn't
bring with me the things I might need.

My second day at the prison I was taken to the infirmary
for a checkup. The doctor was a portly and pleasant man,
and I informed him that I had no toothbrush and I was in the
habit of brushing my teeth before going to bed and when
getting up. He pondered a minute, then went digging into a
cupboard and handed me a new toothbrush. "I can give you
this. But don't tell the others, it's not a standard practise
to give out toothbrushes." I promised not to.

Did anyone ever wonder if I'd set out to commit my crime
with a toothbrush in my pocket just in case?

On the one Sunday I was in the prison I went to mass. I
wasn't impelled by a sudden regeneration of my lapsed
Catholic faith. It was a combination of curiosity—to see
what a mass behind bars was like—and of following the
crowd. There was full attendance. It was one of the few
breaks in the monotony of the week. It's possible an hour
of Devil worship would have drawn the same crowd.

It was more or less an ordinary mass. As is said, when
you've seen one you've seen them all. Except the sermon
was in French. And the congregation was singular, being
a hundred per cent males wearing drabby gray uniforms.
About ten of them went to communion. I found that surprising,
it surfaced an old prejudice which said men in prison had
turned their backs on religion, they scorned it as a pastime
for women and poets. But nobody snickered at the men taking
communion. It was no problem, just a routine affair, not a
sign of weakness or effeminancy. Well, that's good, I
thought. I tried to pick out a few words of the priest's
sermon but was not successful. I asked one of the French
guys—there were a number of them who'd gathered around

to listen to Dan's tales—I asked one of them later what the priest had said.

"Da same ol' ting, you know dat stuff, about repent for your sin an' error of da pas' an' promise not to make dose same mistake again," I was told. "Dat shit about da grace of God an' say your prayer an' da greatness of da Church. You give your prayer an' your soul an' some of your money to da Church, eh? an' God is gone 'elp you, tabernac! An' den he talk about drinking, 'cause you know mos' da guy in da chapel dere drunks an' dere always in 'ere. Like me—dis is da secon' time I'm spending six month in dis 'ole."

The pencil strokes on my cell wall added up.

"You're getting out today," one of the French guys said to me.

"Yeah? You sure?" I was about ready to go too. Despite the diversion of Dan's story telling the routine of the place was extremely boring and the confinement an affront to my free spirit. It was not really a very pleasant spot to be. Those barred windows, the high walls, the public toilets, the stubbly faces, the stale smells, the smoke in the air, the raw throats, the coughing and spitting, the cursing and swearing, the glazed eyes, the heavy boots on the cement, the shouting and hollering in the night, the lonesome fog-horns on the river, the parading in lines, the locking of iron doors, the derelicts, the dead-end youngsters, the shuffling zombies. You can have it.

Around mid-morning I heard my name called by the guard. He's right, this must be it, I thought. But it wasn't, not quite. "You go to the barber," I was told. I didn't want to go to a barber, my hair and beard were doing okay. "Do I have to?" I said.

The barber asked me how I wanted my hair cut. It was a regular barbershop inside the prison. "I hardly want it cut

at all," I said. "Just this much." I showed him my finger
and thumb with about a hundredth of an inch between. So he
made a few clippety-clips with his scissors and pointed me
at the mirror and asked if that was all right. I said it was.
"You can shave yourself if you like," he said.
 "I wouldn't mind giving my beard a slight trim," I said.
"Can I borrow a pair of scissors?" There was a guard in
the room with us.
 "No, we don't allow that," the barber said.
 "I just want to give my beard a little trim."
He exchanged glances with the guard who shook his head.
"Sorry, we can't let you have scissors."
 "I won't attack anyone."
 "Yes, I know, but it's the rule."
 "Okay," I said. "I'll give my neck a little shave. Where's
the razor?"
There were a couple of sinks on the wall, and the barber
pointed out the razor. It was a safety razor, very much a
safety razor. It was attached to the wall by a chain and the
blade was locked in.
When I was finished at the barber's I was escorted back
to the common rooms.
 "It won't be long now," said Dan. "Sorry you have to go,
it was nice talking to you."
 "Well, in a way I'm sorry to be leaving, but not very
much. I enjoyed our conversations a lot myself. I wonder
what time I'll be let out?"
I was impatient. Every second I expected the call to come
for me. I wasn't absolutely sure I *was* getting out today
either, because nothing officially had been told me. It
would be a long evening if there was a mistake.
Dan was talking about becoming a university professor
in the fall. He said he thought he could convince some
university that he had a doctorate. He could forge the papers
and then do some smart talking.

"What would you teach?" I said.

"Theology probably. Comparative religions. Being a professor sounds like a soft job. Running around the way I do I'm wasting my intellect."

At noon we went for dinner, and as I was leaving the dining hall a guard stopped me. "Come with me," he said. We went upstairs and I was told I was being released. My young heart leapt with joy. They gave me my clothes and I took a shower and returned the gray uniform. An old geezer of a man was being released at the same time. He took his shower beside me, his body white and wrinkled. He didn't appear to be the least elated. Leaving to him must have become as routine as arriving. I watched him dress, his street clothes ragged and pathetic. The soles of his shoes were coming off.

At the desk I was given my possessions back, and an itemized account of the tobacco, papers and matches I'd bought, the money having been deducted from my small horde.

"Okay, you can leave by that door. And we don't want to see you back here again," said the sergeant.

"I'll accept that," I said.

I was welcomed by a flood of sunlight and an open street. The trees and grass were as green as could be, it was a clear and perfect day for walking out of jail. I stood for a moment to take it in, only a moment to take a breath of the summer air and soak up the feeling of freedom, and I was on my way.

After a few blocks of brisk walking I looked over my shoulder to see if I was being followed, remembering what Bernard had said. I stopped at a red light and though there was no traffic I stood and waited for the light to turn green, something I had never done in Montreal, and which is not

done by anybody in Montreal or Quebec. But I didn't want
to break the law. I mean I didn't want to get caught breaking
the law and thrown back in jail. The way I felt, my peace
of mind was in proportion to the distance I put between me
and the Quebec Prison. I walked directly to the train station,
going down the little streets on the hill, those fine old
streets which I would not be able to stay around and enjoy.
It would have been delightful to stroll around in the sun
dawdling my way from tavern to tavern, but I wanted to put
Quebec behind me for the time being. In any case I had no
place to stay now. At the station I bought a ticket on the
next train to Montreal—where else was I to go?—leaving in
two hours time. Then I repaired to a nearby alehouse. I
considered calling Bernard, but I didn't want to talk to him
really, not at this time. The best thing, I concluded, was
to write him a letter from Montreal.

FOOTNOTE

   This story took place a few years ago and since that time
the Quebec Prison has ceased to function as a prison.
Some renovations were applied to it and it presently serves
during the summer as a hostel for transient youth.

The Newbridge sighting

FLYING SAUCERS SEEM to be a
common enough sight about the world, judging by what you
read in the papers. The only person I know who ever saw
one was Alec Mooney. Alec was a bachelor of about fifty,
a railroadman, a familiar figure in the Black Horse tavern
and a conversationalist of some renown. The only thing
wrong with his conversation was that he talked so fast he
was almost unintelligible. But he was usually worth
listening to until he got too many in him. Then it was
impossible to understand a word he said.

Alec's job at the CN was shovelling snow in winter. He
may have worked there in the summer, but I don't know.
He said he did. He said he did very important work for the
CNR, winter and summer. He drove the engines and handled
the telegraph service, and he managed the station in Burnley

from time to time. He was moreover a close friend of the
big boss of the railroad, "Mr. CNR," as he called him.
He delivered trains all over Canada for Mr. CNR and helped
formulate policies for the railroad.

He regularly attended important meetings in Montreal
where I believe he was an important member of the Board
of Directors of the CNR.

Besides being a great railroad man, Alec was many other
great things. He was a connoisseur of rum and drank about
two or three quarts a day while on the job, driving the big
engines, but the rum had hardly any effect on him.

"I know how to drink, drink, how to drink, I do, drink
rum, I can, hear that, drink rum, don't feel a thing, I can."

He had to repeat himself when he talked because he
talked so fast he had to come back and pick you up again
so you wouldn't get lost too far behind.

He was, it must also be said, a great lover, and the girls
he seduced while on his runs across Canada would make
Casanova blush with shame by comparison.

Alec wore a finely trimmed moustache which gave him a
distinctive, rather debonair appearance. He normally had
on a railroad cap, but when he was dressed smartly he wore
a black tam. He was tall with a rugged weather-beaten
face, and looked like a sincere and honest man. You would
have to believe him if he said he saw a flying saucer. I
mean, if you had holes in your head you'd believe him.

But all the same, he was the first man in Newbridge who
even claimed he saw a saucer. It was in the tavern that he
made his announcement.

"You know them flying saucer things, flying saucers,
saucers, eh, you know them flying saucers, flying saucers?"

"What about them, Alec?" said Paul Ryan, looking over
the top of his beer. "You been seeing flying saucers,
Alec?" he said.

"Damn right, damn right, I saw one, I did, saw one last

night I did."

"Aw, go on, Alec, you're full of shit."

"I did, I did, yes I did, the truth, Ryan, the truth by God, I saw one last, last, last night, I did."

Jimmy Skidd, who was sitting with us, said:

"Where'd you see it, Alec? Was there any little green men in it?"

"Didn't see any green men, I didn't, no green men, but I saw the flying saucer you bet by God, yes, yes, I saw it, saw it last night."

"Where'd you see it, Alec, now tell us that?"

"Out by the ball diamond, ball diamond, eh, yes, right there in the ball diamond, it came down, came down, it did, and landed right in the infield. How about that now, eh, flying saucer it was, couldn't have been anything else, anything else, nope, saucer, right in the infield."

"Alec, you're right out of your mind. Flying saucers. Did you go for a trip in it?"

"Don't be smart, don't be smart, Ryan. I know. I know. I saw the flying saucer, I did."

Alec stuck to his story, but that wasn't unusual because he always did, regardless of what he was saying. If he'd said he'd been on the moon that afternoon he wouldn't have denied it even if he'd been in that same chair all day.

"There must be marks on the ball diamond, Alec," said Terry. "A big flying saucer couldn't land right there in the infield and not leave some tracks."

Alec paused a second and said, "Of course, tracks, there's marks, of course, certainly, marks on the ground, yes, it left marks, yes it did."

"Why didn't you tell the cops?"

"Maybe tracks gone now, you don't know. Can't tell cops, don't be crazy, what do cops know, mounties don't know nothing. They'd arrest me for telling lies, wouldn't believe me, believe me, you know the mounties, can't trust them.

No, not saying anything, I'm not."

"Alec, you just made that story up. You didn't see any flying saucer any more than I did."

But Alec was adamant. He cursed and swore at Ryan for not believing him, and said Ryan didn't know anything about anything.

"Alright, Alec, why don't you tell the newspapers about your saucer," Ryan said. "All kinds of crackpots are always telling the papers about seeing saucers, so you might as well get your two cents in."

"Going to, going to," said Alec, nodding his head swiftly and tossing down a drink of beer. "Yes, yes. Moncton *Times*, *Times* man called me up and wants story, wants to know all about it. Interview, he wants, he does, interview. Going to talk to man from the *Times*, I am."

"Well, that's great," said Terry, "we should read about it in tomorrow's paper."

"Maybe, maybe, but you can't tell, can't tell. They might want to keep it secret, secret, government business you know, saucers, government business. Outer space, attack from outer space maybe, maybe, got to keep it quiet. Talk to man from the *Times* and we'll see, we will."

He nodded his head knowingly.

"Aw, that's all baloney," said Ryan.

"Go to hell, Ryan, go to hell, hell, hell with you, Ryan," said Alec.

After all hands had quaffed a few more beers and Alec was still claiming he'd seen a flying saucer and that it had landed on the infield of the baseball diamond, Ryan suggested that we go look for the marks the saucer left.

"Don't be crazy," I said. "We're not going to walk all the way out to the ball park just to look for flying saucer tracks."

"Maybe Alec really saw a flying saucer," said Ryan. "How do we know? He's probably just the kind who sees them."

"Yeah, that's about the size of it."

"I don't know," said Ryan, tipping his glass. "If there weren't saucers flying around all these people wouldn't be reporting them every day."

"Well, you can go look for tracks if you like."

"Honestly now, Alec," said Ryan, "did you really see a flying saucer last night?"

Ryan was one of those inscrutable people that you never know is being serious or pulling somebody's leg. He never laughed, no matter what he or anybody else said, so you couldn't tell what was going on in his mind. But most of the time he wasn't serious about anything he said.

"What were you doing up by the ball park last night anyway?" he asked Alec.

"Looking it over, over, I was, looking the field over. Might coach ball team next season, asked me to, they did, want me to coach the All-Stars. Got to check the field, that's what I was doing, eh, check the field, might coach team. Saw flying saucer, came down, whooosh, came down, it did, just out of nowhere, all bright and shining, whooosh, down on the field, almost scared me to death, I was."

"And then it just flew away?"

"Oh, about two minutes, two minutes it was on the field, two minutes, three minutes, and windows, windows in it, see, and all lit up, windows, and I saw queer-looking guy, strange, like a monster, peeping out the window—"

"You never said that before," said Terry. "You mean you saw one of these outer space creatures?"

"Sure, I did, I did, yes, I did, saw him in the window, head there, head, colored orange, orange sort of, see, orange, crazy-looking guy, man from Mars probably."

"There you go, now," said Ryan. "If Alec can describe things in that detail, then they must be true."

"Goddam right, damn right, Ryan."

"We might be in for an invasion," said Ryan.

"That's the truth, truth, that is, by God, see."

Then Ryan said that the only thing to be done was the newspapers must hear about this sighting. He ordered another round of beer and said we'd have to call the Moncton *Times* and give them the story.

"This could make Alec famous," he said. "The first UFO sighting in Norwich county."

"What about Alec's interview with the *Times* man?" said Terry.

"We can't wait for that. We have to get Alec on the phone right now with the story. The interview might be too late. Someone else is liable to see the saucer and Alec would miss his chance."

By now Alec was on his eighth or ninth pint and Ryan was telling him to drink up. Alec's capacity was on the limited side, and he was clearly feeling the effects of what he'd drunk. He was grinning foolishly and nodding his head to everything Ryan said.

"We'll get you on the phone and you give the story to the *Times*," Ryan was saying. "You'll be a big man after this."

"Right, Ryan, right, Ryan, big man, I am."

There was a pay phone in the tavern just inside the entrance and we all got up and gathered around it.

"Just tell your story, nice and straightforward," said Ryan, dialling the number.

He dropped the money in for the call and got hold of the newsroom. "Hello, I have a story that might be of interest to you," he said. "A man here in Newbridge has seen a flying saucer . . . Yes, that's right, a flying saucer. His name's Alec Mooney, an employee of the CNR . . . It landed on the infield of the Newbridge ball park . . . That's right, no kidding, he got a firsthand look at it, Alec Mooney's his name . . . about 9:30 tonight . . . yes, he's

here. He's very excited about it, he saw one of the
creatures in the machine to . . . Yes, here he is . . . he's
very nervous, he can hardly get control of himself, but I'll
put him on."

Alec was pushed onto the telephone and began to relate
the details of his sighting. What he gave was a thorough
enough description, only it's unlikely the guy at the other
end got a single word out of it. But Alec went on a mile a
minute until he had his story out, and then Ryan took the
phone again.

"You get all that?" he said. "What did you say? . . .
Yes, he speaks English . . . I know, he's just very
shook-up about it all, almost in a state of shock, I'd say,
but it's the real thing . . . Mr. Mooney is a well-known
citizen of Newbridge, and if he says he saw a flying saucer
you can be sure it's the truth . . . It was at the Newbridge
ball park, around 9:30 this evening . . . The ship he saw
was round, about 60 feet in diameter, and it was glowing
all over, and in a window he saw one of the passengers . . .
that's right, he was orange coloured and had some kind of
ugly horns sticking out and one big eye in the middle of
his forehead, and he—or it, or whatever it was—was bald as
an egg . . . The saucer stayed about three minutes . . .
Mr. Mooney was hiding behind the backstop, and then it
took off, faster than the eye could follow . . . Traces? Oh
yes, there are marks out on the field where it landed. This
has been confirmed by Mr. Mooney, and an investigative
team from the Air Force base is expected to look at them
tomorrow . . . that about covers it . . . yes, that's about
it . . . Yes, I believe there were other witnesses, but I
don't have their names at the moment . . . Certainly, Mr.
Mooney would be glad to see a reporter tomorrow. We
expect he'll be seeing many reporters . . . I'm a friend of
Mr. Mooney's, I've known him since we were kids, I'll be
only too happy to vouch for anything he says—pardon me,

it's getting very busy around here, you can hear the noise . . . I'm sorry, some officials have just arrived. You've got everything? . . . all right . . . in tomorrow's paper. Good . . . fine, goodbye . . . pardon me? . . . yes, fine now, I have to go . . . thank you very much, I hope you've got everything right . . . that's right . . . tomorrow. Goodbye."

Ryan hung up and said: "Time for another round."

The next day the story appeared on the bottom half of the front page. It was headlined: **UFO in Newbridge?** The story went on to say:

A mysterious flying object was reported to have landed in Newbridge last evening.

Witnesses to the incident say the strange craft set down in the local ball park and remained there several minutes before suddenly taking off with blinding speed.

Mr. Alec Mooney, an employee of the CN and one of those who made the sighting, described the object to this paper last night.

In a state bordering on nervous shock, Mr. Mooney said: "I never believed in flying saucers before, so you can imagine the start it gave me.

"This thing was about sixty feet in diameter and shaped round, and part of it seemed to rotate when it was in motion.

"From where I stood I could see windows, like portholes, in the machine and looking out one of these windows was an unusual creature.

"He was orange coloured and his skin glowed, like there was a light inside him, and on his head there were two horn-like

objects, possibly antennae.
"It was horrible."
Authorities are in the process of
investigating the incident.
The sighting is the first reported
in the Newbridge area and has all
citizens out looking for the possible
return of the ship.

The article caused a considerable stir in Newbridge, and
by mid-afternoon half the town was up at the ball field to
see where the saucer had landed.

The opinion of most of the citizens, as they made their
way to the ball park, went something like this: "That crazy
Mooney, he's made up stories about everything else, and
now he's gone so far as to get himself into the papers with
a story of flying saucers." All the same they went to look.

And when they got to the park their skepticism changed
to wonder, and then even to belief. Because out on the ball
field protected by a cordon set up by the RCMP were, in
fact, the marks left by the strange machine from outer
space.

Three depressions in the earth, one between first base
and second, one at shortstop, and one between third base
and home plate.

"There might really have been one, you never know,"
they whispered. "How else can you explain those marks out
there."

It was adjudged that the marks were made by tripod
landing gear. Authorities from the RCAF base near town
duly arrived to check the markings, and Alec was
immediately located for questioning.

"Very strange," said one of the Air Force officers.
"Could be a hoax, but what motive could he have for
inventing all this? *Something* he saw seems to have addled

his brain.''

When interviewed Alec stuck to his story. He had seen the saucer, it had landed, he'd seen a man in it, and then it had taken off.

Did it have tripod landing gear, he was asked.

"What's that, what, what, sure it landed, landed, I am.''

It was explained to him what the landing gear was, and he said, "Don't know, how could I know, dark, dark it was, couldn't tell, sure it had landing gear, gear, had to, had to land, eh, it came in, came in it did and landed on the infield, I saw it, I did.''

Alec's picture appeared in the *Times* next day and he was instantly a famous man around the county, and the Air Force officers stopped questioning him because to begin with they could scarcely understand what he was saying. And he seemed to say all things at once, so they didn't know what to make of him.

Samples of the earth on the ball diamond were taken and sent to the Federal laboratories in Ottawa. All ball games on the field were suspended as though it was sacred ground, and the town council considered designating it an official tourist attraction. But after a few days the park was in use again, because there was nowhere else to play ball, and the schedule was getting held up. Tourists, if they liked, could still look at the place where the saucer landed, when there wasn't a game going on.

Some time later a report came back from Ottawa saying there was nothing whatever that could be deduced from the sand from the ball park. It was just ordinary sand, and there was no radioactivity or pieces of metal or anything. There was just nothing.

But that didn't prove there wasn't a space ship. It merely meant that if there was, it had left no traces aside from the indentations of its landing gear.

A few months after the sighting the same bunch of us were

sitting around a table at the Black Horse. Alec was telling
us that he'd just got back from Toronto where he'd been
talking with Mr. CNR who was hinting about retiring soon.

"See, Mr. CNR, he says Alec, Alec, he says, got to
retire, retire one of these days, see, he says, and I says
yes, Mr. CNR, you're getting old, getting old, I said, I did,
and he says, Alec, Alec, Alec, we need a new man, new
man he says, to run railroad. New man, see. Yes, I says,
yes, need a new man, I says. Alec, Alec, he says, how'd
you like run the railroad, run railroad, he says, he did,
said to me, Alec, how'd you like run the railroad, railroad,
run the railroad, he said, and I says, well, don't know,
don't know, eh, don't know says I, busy, busy these days,
busy. Air Force after me, Air Force, I says, Air Force
want me work on flying saucers, see, says I, flying saucers,
know all about them, I do, maybe next year, Mr. CNR,
maybe next year, take the job, maybe, I will."

"D'you do much travelling now that you're famous,
Alec?" said Skidd.

"Oh yes, oh yes, never stop, not me, on the go all the
time. Got a lot of business, business, I have."

"How are the women treating you?"

"Don't mention it, women, oh, yes, should've see the
blonde, blonde, blonde in Toronto, built like this, like this,
see," and with a sly look he shaped out the measurements
with his hands. "She said, blonde said, Alec, should be a
movie star, she said, that's right, Alec, she said, should
be in movies, well, I led her on, I did, led her on, led her
on, looked like Marilyn Monroe, better, better though, Alec,
she says, how'd you like come to my place for a drink of
rum, rum, see, and . . ."

And Alec went on to describe his evening with girl in
Toronto. At length Ryan said:

"Seen any more flying saucers, Alec?"

"Nope, no more, not since last one, no, none lately.

Showed you, eh, Ryan, didn't believe me, flying saucer, didn't believe me, eh? You saw, saw the tracks, place where tripod landed, eh?"

He laughed and poured down a good drink of hi beer.

"I know what I saw, I know, can't fool me," he said. "Yep, flew right in, it did, flying saucer, from Mars likely, landed in ball park. Didn't believe me, did you, Ryan? Showed you, ha, showed you, I did. Yes sir, space ship, landed right in Newbridge."

Of course what Ryan had done that night was gone up to the park with a shovel and made those three holes. But all he said was:

"By God, Alec, I'll never doubt your word again."

"Taught you, eh Ryan, showed you, I did, yes sir."

On the bus

THE INCIDENT I'M about to relate is of such minor significance that I doubt anyone but myself would bother relating it. I've wracked my brain to find a moral behind it. If I found a moral then it would not seem such a waste of time.

One thing about morals is they are always summed up in catchy little phrases like "everybody loves a winner," which to begin with is a lie because I don't love winners. I love losers, failures, flops, non-successes. There is a common bond between flops and myself because I am one, even though I am still a young man. You may consider me too young to be dismissed outright as a flop. Nevertheless

I am a flop because I know I'm a flop, and those who
consider themselves flops are generally successful at being
flops.

I don't want to get too far astray. Aside from establishing
an ungainly writing style I've written a paragraph that has
little or nothing to do with what I want to say—and I would
like to make *more* irrelevant remarks. My mind wanders
badly at all times. I have a deplorable time concentrating;
my interest in anything worthwhile, I mean anything that
pays dividends as the world understands them, is fleeting
at best.

You understand, then, why it is virtually impossible for
me to be any kind of success.

Yesterday I learned the horrible truth, namely, that my
days as a scholar were over. It was a lovely warm April
afternoon, it would have been a nice day for a nice surprise,
but this is not the age of miracles. McGill was teeming
with depressingly cheerful drones who had passed their
year. But I had failed mine miserably. This news did not
come as a surprise to me. How could it have been otherwise
when my mind is forever drifting, entertaining daydreams,
imaginary love affairs, playing with the lines of a poem,
the contours of a painting, scenes from a film, technicolor
pictures of myself as a dashingly heroic, imposing and
scintillating figure? In reality I am not heroic or scintillating or any of those other words. In appearance I am
nondescript—slightly ugly but not enough to draw attention—
my mind is not brilliant, I rarely say witty things, I suspect
that I am frequently boring the people I talk to.

I can see forming in your mind, Aha, you say, I have this
young fellow pegged, he is at heart a romantic, an artist,
and he blames himself for failing to pass his courses in
engineering which his stern father forced him to take—but
you are wrong, my courses were in art and literature, things
which interest me although I am unable to *study* them or

respond in the proper scholarly tradition. Nor do I have any talent in my own right as an artist of any kind. I am modest, I understand myself, I am a would-be painter, a would-be poet, a would-be film maker, a would-be actor, a would-be singer, and yes, a would-be lover. I do none of these things well nor have I ever given the creative aspect of my life any large attention. I accept what I am: a dilettante, a middleclass dilettante.

I am one with—let me repeat—flops because they remind me of myself, my sympathies go out strongly to them, they are my brothers, we are all destined to muddle along in life. I expect I will succeed in holding down some insignificant job throughout my life, using what money I put aside to buy books, the occasional painting, to attend a concert, the movies, to have my small pleasures. I am capable of accepting my condition in reality—even if I continue to allow myself to indulge in fruitless fantasies.

But for all my self adjustment, to assume I was serene as I walked off the campus of McGill and along noisy Sherbrooke street would be a grave mistake. I had used up my last chance as a student, I could not return to McGill now nor to any other university because I had failed far too many courses over the past four years. I should have finished in three years and yet I had stumbled on for four, propping myself up with night credits, those I was able to acquire. But now the end had been reached. I had flunked the entire year. They would not take me back. And if I wished to attend another university it would mean sorting out the pieces of the McGill disaster and beginning somewhere in the second year. This was impossible. It was not just a question of admitting I wasn't cut out to be a scholar, though that is certainly the case, but more than that I could not, I cannot possibly afford to continue as a student. I am more than seven thousand dollars in debt. Over the past four years I've lived on government loans,

bank loans, and loans from my family. Very soon I have to
start paying this money back. The bank is charging interest,
the government will commence doing so if I don't begin
paying shortly, and I am morally obliged to repay my father
and brother. Neither is wealthy, far from it. They live in
Moncton (which I find a depressing city, by the way, very
philistine) where my father is assistant manager of Eaton's
rug department and my older brother Ronald a salesman on
the same floor. I am the scholar in the family, or was until
yesterday. They thought I would do well. I once thought I
would do well myself. I *used* to do well, but something
happened to me towards the end of high school, the interest
in studies I once had faded. I believe I was at my peak at
the age of seventeen and then apathy set in. It was only
momentum that carried me off to Montreal and McGill and
that momentum decreased daily until now I am standing
still, a failed scholar. I would like to explain why this
happened, where this indifference came from, why I just
could not give myself to my studies, but I'm not sure I can.
It may stem from—I don't know what. I don't wish to pursue
success, I shy from obligations, I want to have been born
rich and able to live the dilettante's life in proper fashion.
   You might ask, How could I borrow so much money and
leave myself in the position of letting my family down
badly? The answer is this: it's because I enjoyed my life
as a student, as a student in the way I was a student.
For four years I came and went more or less as I pleased,
pausing only now and then to acknowledge the existence
of my studies, working only when I absolutely had to in
order to extend my way of life. It had to catch up with me.
It did so yesterday. Hence, as I said, I was not entirely
happy as I walked along Sherbrooke with McGill behind me
forever. I knew this day had to arrive, the halcyon years
had to end, and like my father and brother I would also
climb onto the treadmill. Would I work in Eaton's rug

department? The thought made me shudder.

I could have berated myself for having been such a loafer, for if I had applied myself I might perhaps have graduated and pursued post-graduate studies and continued as a student possibly all my life. But that was no solution because, to begin with, the academic treadmill is not much different from any other. They expect you to labour over some pointless pursuit, and they're forever looking over your shoulder to see you don't relax. And I would be expected to teach courses and I'd hate that. It was impossible for me to do other than what I did. I could not, for love nor money, apply myself to the degree necessary to succeed. I lived each day for itself. What might happen tomorrow was not my concern.

I crossed Peel street and stopped before the windows of the Gallery Martal. There were a few paintings as usual by Bernard Buffet in the window, but that's not why I mention stopping here. My reason is that I am going to use a literary device. As I stood before the large window I saw a reflection of my own person.

It was warm yesterday so I wasn't wearing a coat. The month is April (how do authors handle this irksome problem of "is" and "was" when the past is only yesterday?). I was wearing a pair of faded blue jeans and a gray sweat-shirt, comfortable clothes but nothing to make you turn your head. My hair, as is the style, was (is?) shoulder length. These days not only students but even businessmen it seems wear their hair that way. You'll see the implication of my hair later, and how absurd is the incident I am going to describe. Because I am nearsighted I wear glasses, they are ordinary wire-rimmed glasses. And then there's my size. I am a little over average height and a bit on the portly side. Not much, but perhaps a few pounds overweight as

the result of a good appetite and the sedentary life I lead.
I have always had an aversion to any exercise aside from
walking.

Now that you have my description I can walk away from
the windows of Gallery Martal.

It might be safe to say that my earlier remark about the
state of my spirits was an understatement. I said I wasn't
happy. The truth is, I was distressed, I was depressed.
This is understandable because what had I to look forward
to? Some manner of drudgery—if I could find it. A perfect
case of bitter irony. According to the newspapers employment was scarce, so I would be forced to seek out
diligently that which I did not want at all. It was like
making the condemned man build his own gallows. I had no
idea where I could start. On occasion, during moments of
uncommon fortitude and anticipating my present position, I
had let my eyes wander over the classified ads in the *Star*.
I saw many jobs but every one of them made my heart sink.
There are no jobs that I know of designed to satisfy persons
who do not want to have a job.

As I walked along Sherbrooke, on the bank of a river of
roaring traffic, so to speak, I pondered what I could do to
make myself feel better. "Doom. Doom lies ahead," I
thought. "Tomorrow I walk down a dark corridor at the end
of which there is no light. But . . . that is tomorrow. Today,
I will live one last day before giving myself up to slavery."

My bank is at the corner of Sherbrooke and Guy, for I live
only one block up the hill on McGregor. I went into the bank
and withdrew a hundred dollars. That left in my account
fifty-six dollars and thirty-two cents, not much at all, but
then it was part of tomorrow's life, a life of trials and
tribulations. Today it could not concern me.

No doubt another person in my place would have proceeded

to get blindly drunk, that being the traditional course
followed by men as hopeless as myself. I do not generally
drink but I made a gesture, a somewhat grand gesture in
that direction by going directly to the Mountain Street
Liquor Store and buying a bottle of champagne.

Let us now glance into the hypothetical future, the
immediate future as I envisioned it at that moment. You see
me thus, several hours later, sprawled languorously in my
easy chair at home admiring my new Baeschlen on the wall,
sipping pink champagne, cigaret held lightly in my fingers,
while in the background a Chopin *ballade* plays gently on
my stereo. From time to time I rise and go to the kitchen
where gradually a meal fit for royalty is coming into
existence under the tutelage of my expert fingers. The
afternoon blends into evening tenderly . . .

This, I remind you, was merely the picture I had in my
mind. More important, it was another literary device, this
time to divulge how I spent my hundred dollars.

The painting was the largest extravagance but the easiest
to indulge myself in because, of course, a painting is
always an investment, isn't it? Although you can never tell
with these things. If it's an investment you're making you
had better become more acquainted with the artist's contacts
than his work. There are many painters around. Karl
Baeschlen has no reputation yet, and may never have. But
it was because of this I could afford one of his works. I
was, I am, much impressed by his talent, splendid pieces
of a surrealistic—but stop—this is not important, in fact it
has nothing whatever to do with the incident I'm trying to
get around to. As far as you are concerned the *size* of the
painting is the important thing. It was five feet tall by
three feet wide. With frame it cost me seventy-five dollars.
As I handed over the money to pay for it there stood beside
me on the gallery floor a bag of rather expensive foods
carefully selected shortly before from various delicatessens

for the sumptuous meal I envisioned. Leaning against the bag of food was a thin square package which anyone could tell was a longplaying record, though in fact it was *two* longplaying records (like most romantics I love Chopin, and these were additions to my collection of the works of that great man). And of course there was my bottle of champagne.

My hundred dollars was gone. I could have bought a less expensive Baeschlen, they started at fifty dollars, but then I would not have got the one I wanted.

I now had fifty-six cents in my pocket. This, unfortunately, was insufficient for a taxi home. I was in the Labyrinth Gallery, one of a number of crudely thrown together basement boutiques operated by a collection of young persons, the type some individuals persist in calling "hippies," though I consider the word much out of fashion. However, my views are not always shared by everyone, I know in the minds of some people it is still a living word, it serves as a handy generalization. You will see.

The Labyrinth is on Saint Catherine just west of Bleury, almost next door to the Parisien Theatre.

I could, I said to myself, gathering my unwieldy assortment of possessions into my arms, take the Metro to Guy street, then transfer to a bus. But that seemed not the best way, because it meant going through turnstiles and up and down stairs and on and off a subway car as well as a bus. It was simpler, I concluded, to walk down to Dorchester and take one of the three buses that ran along Dorchester turning north at Guy and on up to my street which is McGregor. It would not be as quick as the Metro, but it would be far easier.

It's not such a short walk to the nearest stop on Dorchester and the going was extremely awkward. I had to halt every few paces and adjust my burden. The afternoon had grown quite hot and by the time I reached the bus stop

I was perspiring and angry at myself for doing things in what was obviously the wrong way. On the surface I was attempting to make a joyful day of it, but walking around like a pack mule should not have been part of the plot. One day you should try carrying a five-by-three-foot painting, two LP-records, a heavy quart of champagne and a bulky bag of groceries as far as I did. Although the bus route was along Dorchester and that was only one block from Saint Catherine, the nearest stop was located in front of Place Ville Marie, another three blocks west.

I don't personally know that many elderly people but if you had asked me what I thought of them as a rule, most probably my reply would have been, "Well, I believe I like them, they're over the hill and not so aggressive, they've seen a good deal of life and I expect they are wiser than they used to be. They are slow moving, I like their pace."
     If there's one thing I've always detested it's a person who takes up two seats on a bus.
     The scene opens with me climbing onto the 65 bus with my painting, groceries, records and bottle of champagne. I had my ticket out and ready and with a little flick of thumb and forefinger, the only two parts of my body available, and these only partly so, I dropped the ticket into the slot and sat down. I sat on the long sideseat at the front nearest the door. There was nobody else on this seat which was designed to hold four bodies.
     Now that I was seated a casual observer would see me thus: a young gentleman with records and champagne (both in wrappers) on his lap, an enormous painting (also wrapped but fooling nobody) standing in front of him and hugged in close to his knees, and a large bag of groceries on the seat beside him, a tall loaf of French bread sticking out the top. He had his left hand on this bag keeping it

snug against his side.

As the sun glinted off the windows of the skyward-
reaching office buildings along Dorchester the bus glided
forward stopping at Mansfield, Drummond, Bishop, Guy,
then rounding the corner at Guy and travelling northward
and upward. Looking out the expansive front windshield
I saw ahead the great brick pile of the Montreal General
Hospital, assorted towering apartment buildings, a part of
the mountain, the busy crossroads at Guy and Saint
Catherine. At the different stops we took on new
passengers. At Bishop, for example, two oldish women got
on and sat on the long seat beside me. They appeared to
have just come from a beauty parlour, their gray hair was
propped up smartly on their heads, their wrinkled faces
were made up carefully with pink powder. They were
dressed quite well and they both wore little black gloves.
The seat looked like this: the two women, a little space,
then me and my supplies squeezed up against the end of
the seat. The women sat there sniffing, at any rate they
seemed to me to be sitting there sniffing.

On the green light we crossed Saint Catherine and pulled
up in front of the Metro station at Maisonneuve. The door
hissed open and feet clomped up onto the bus, tickets
were dropped into the slot, transfers changed hands, small
change clattered into the box. The mouth of the Metro
station disgorged more humans who climbed onto the bus.
The bus was filling up, but a glance to my left showed me
there were still a few seats at the back. The door shut
and we moved off, getting jammed into the traffic before
reaching Sherbrooke and being forced to inch along.

There was a man standing in front of me, I could see
him over the top of my painting. He was in his late fifties,
a sharp-faced man with bulging eyes.

"Would you move over, don't take two places," he said.

But I was not taking two places, I was taking a place

and a half, and this was obviously because of all the things
I had with me. I pulled my bag of groceries closer, I pressed
harder against the end of the seat. The man sat down,
squeezing himself in.

"Why don't you put that bag on your knee," he said.
"People want to sit down."

"I've got things on my knee," I said. "And I have to
hold my painting."

"Some people think they own the seats on these buses,"
he said.

"You've got a seat," I said. "What more do you want?"

Suddenly the two old women were talking, and loudly.
"What do you expect from that kind?" said one. This was
followed by a remark that, if it were not true, I would never
think of making up. "Dirty hippie," she said. I couldn't
quite believe my ears.

"It's about time someone stood up to them," said the
other.

"Some of these characters think they own the world,"
the man said out of the side of his mouth, the side the
women were on.

The bus was absolutely silent except for the speakers.

"Look at that hair. Did you ever see anything like it?"
said one of the women.

"It's disgraceful. Something should be done about them."

"They'd all be in jail if I had anything to say about it."

"Disgusting. If one of my grandchildren ever got like that
I'd skin him alive."

"Oh, and I would too. They shouldn't allow them on the
streets."

"It's disgusting."

I was a witness to what followed. You will understand I
was driven to it. You can envision me sitting there having
to hear myself vilified in such a fashion, and so unjustly,
and with a full bus straining their ears to catch every word,

and they didn't have to strain hard because my seat
companions *meant* to be heard by everyone. The bus had
crossed Sherbrooke and was moving up Cote des Neiges
Road (which is still Guy Street but the name changes at
this point, if you didn't know that), and they kept babbling
away and pouring out venom on me relentlessly, and everyone was staring at me.

The man was squeezed in beside me and making little
comments sideways at the old women, agreeing with all
they said and adding his own brilliant observations and
no doubt feeling very heroic for having stood up to the
hippie menace. All of a sudden I shot my hand across his
face and up, passing an inch from his nose, and reaching
as if to pull the stop cord. He jumped about a foot off his
seat. "I thought this was my stop," I said, withdrawing
my hand. In fact it *was* my stop, we were coming to
McGregor, but I didn't ring the bell. Instead I started
sniffing loudly. Then I boomed out in the biggest voice I
could manage:

"Listen, for God's sake, I don't like to bring this up,
but mister—don't you ever *wash?* You smell *terrible*, I
mean, you *stink!* When was the last time you *washed?*
This has been *torture* sitting here, are you sure you didn't
die a few months ago?"

His jaw fell, he was so startled to hear this, then he
turned a couple of shades of purple. He started to reply
but the incongruity had confused him, since it was
supposed to be *him* talking about *me* being filthy. It caught
him offstride. "You—you—don't you talk about washing—
hippies—filthy bum—you—you—this—" meaningless
mutterings like that. Naturally the women were exclaiming
"well I never" and "of all the nerve!"

"And you too," I boomed, while I was at it. "My golly,
you'd think ladies your age would learn something about
cleanliness. Look at you, you get on a public conveyance

and you stink like *a pair of old drawers*. Didn't you ever
smell yourselves? Look at the dirt on your faces, the lines
are *caked* with *scruff*. Honestly, a little *wash* every now
and then—"

At this they commenced screaming and howling and
setting up a terrible protest, faces contorted and murderous.
All three were going together, they were so outraged and
indignant, they had never been so downright mortified.
While their counter-insults got jumbled up with each other
I was carrying on in a great heavy voice saying things like:

"I certainly wouldn't let *my* parents out on the street in
your condition, it should be a *crime* to subject innocent
people like myself to such *rank body odors*. It's *disgusting*,
that's what it is. Have you no sense of *propriety*? Are you
so *oblivious* to the senses of others? Do you actually *like*
to be so dirty and smell so bad? It's enough to make a
person *throw up!*"

And they were still squawking away— *"I've never heard
we do not smell I'll have you know I took a bath before I left
home this morning don't bother with him the impudent you're the
one who stinks look at you long filthy hair young bum I wash
every day she doesn't smell never been so insulted do I smell
bad tell me do I smell bad something should be done about how
dare I never heard—"*

I clamped my fingers onto my nose and stuck my tongue
out. "I'm going to *puke*," I said. "I'm going to puke all
over you." The little man beside me went into a panic, he
was squeezed in tight and he tried to bolt up but couldn't
move. "No, wait—it's okay," I said. "I can hold it. I'll
hold my nose, I can't breathe this stench any longer. I think
I'd better get off next stop before I suffocate."

"I ought to—ought to—I ought to—" the man was saying,
quivering and expostulating like a deranged person.

One astonishing thing about all this was the bus driver.
He was sitting only a few feet away and never once turned

his head but continued driving on. I heard one of the women demanding that I be ejected from the bus but he paid no attention. As for the other passengers, before getting off I gave a quick look back at them. There were indifferent expressions and a good many hostile ones. I decided I would accept the indifferents as being on my side, though it's highly likely I was alone in my fight, for who can have sympathy for a youth who insults his elders?

Spanish Jack

THERE WERE THREE English sailors, you see, and they were off a pulp boat down at the Station Wharf, this boat was finishing loading up and the sailors were on shore and they went to the Black Horse, which happens to be the only tavern in town. They were drinking beer and starting to feel pretty good and they were talking in that English kind of accent so you could hardly understand them. But nobody took offence because sailors were common enough around town during the summer, there was always a boat in loading pulp, they came from all over the world, Germany, Italy, Ireland, Norway, England, all with different colours of flags and all the sailors talking foreign languages. You could partly understand the English guys but you had to pay close attention and even then it was hard to get all the words no matter how close you listened.

Jack McIntyre, the old guy who owns the tugboat, was in the Black Horse too, you'd see him there every day, he'd come in about four in the afternoon and sometimes he'd go home for supper, and sometimes he'd stay right through till closing time at 11:30 and then go home. By that time he'd be pretty drunk. It was amazing how he could keep it up because he was more than 75 years old. Most of the time he had a stub of a cigar in his mouth, it might have been the same cigar all the time, because it was never lit and was always the same length, about two inches long. And he had stubbly whiskers, like two or three days growth of beard, and that seemed to stay the same too, which seems impossible, but I don't think I ever saw him clean shaven or with his whiskers any longer. He'd been operating the tugboat for probably fifty years, it looked like the same boat, a worn-out old tub. It was called *Flora*, after his wife. They'd been married probably fifty years, she was about the same age as Jack. You didn't see her much. She stayed in the house most of the time, sometimes she'd come out to buy the groceries. She was scrawny and wrinkled like people get at her age. Some people say she used to be a very goodlooking woman when she was young, and Jack was even supposed to have been quite a goodlooking fellow too, but you couldn't tell it to look at either of them now. You often hear that about old people, how strong they once were, or how smart they were, or how much work they could do in a day, things like that.

Well, Jack was in the Black Horse, and he was sitting beside the English sailors who were drinking beer pretty hard and doing a lot of talking, everything "bloody this and bloody that", and after a while one of them turned to Jack and said, "Hey mate, where can you get a piece of tail in this bloody town?" or something like that, because they'd been talking about skin, like you hear a lot of in taverns, how much they'd got in different ports, and how rough it was being on a ship in the middle of the ocean and having to do without a woman. They were young guys.

"What's that?" said Jack, who didn't understand because of the accent.

"We're tryin' to get bloody laid," the guy repeated. "Where can we find some nice birds," which was their word for girls.

When Jack finally understood them he said: "I don't know nothin' about that, not at my age, my skinnin' days is over," he said.

Well, the English guys laughed, and they bought Jack a beer, because they thought if they weren't going to get laid at least they could have some fun with this old guy.

"What d'you mean, you're too bloody old?" they said. "There's guys ninety years old still doin' it five bloody times a night. I heard of one old bastard who knocked his wife up when he was a hundred."

"Well, I don't know about that," said Jack, "maybe it's true, I don't like to say it ain't to your face, but all I know is I'd just as soon sit back and drink my beer and then go home to bed. I'll leave the skinnin' around to the youngsters. My old woman's a bit past her prime too."

The sailors wouldn't let him off with that. They said if Jack got his hands on a young girl, some real fine looking stuff about eighteen he'd soon forget how old he was.

"Now that might be so," said Jack, "but where am I gonna find a girl of eighteen? The only whore in town is Ma Murphy and she's damn near as old as I am. And you wouldn't catch me goin' near her anyhow, I ain't lookin' to get the clap. If you boys want to give her a try I'll tell you where she lives."

"How bleedin' old is she?"

"Oh, she'd be . . . I guess she'd be around fifty-five, fifty-six. She's a little hard on the eyes too, I might warn ya."

"The hell with that," one of them said.

"She might be better than nothin'," said another one. "If you're drunk enough you don't know the difference."

Well, they talked on about what they would do, and they bought Jack more beer, so he hung around most of the evening, not bothering to go home for supper.

As Jack got feeling better he became more free and talkative on the subject of skin, and he related tales from the past, some of which might have been true and others of which probably weren't. And after a while he began saying things like, "I still got a bit of the tomcat left in me, despite me age. I ain't all I was but I ain't exactly washed up yet either."

And the sailors said why didn't he put the works to his wife when he went home? "She's probably bloody-well starvin' for a good piece of ass," they said.

"Well, I don't know, it's been quite a while and it might come as a shock to her. She's liable to drop dead from shock."

"It'd do the old bird good."

"Well, maybe so, but there's another thing. The wife's a fine enough woman and she was once something to look at but she's gettin' on and a woman loses some of her physical looks with age, if you see what I mean. I don't know if I could still get it up for her, good a woman as she is. Now if she was maybe twenty or thirty years younger I would rush home right this instant and make her happy."

The sailors looked at each other. They grinned. Finally one of them said, "Old man, I got just the bloody thing for you, it'll make your old prick stand up like a bloody ramrod, and it'll make your wife look like a sixteen year old virgin."

"What would that be?" said Jack. A look of suspicion came into his eye.

"You ever hear about Spanish Fly?"

"You're damn right I did. But I don't believe it. And if I

did I wouldn't touch the stuff. I heard stories, but I never
seen it, and I never believed the stories because people
are always making things up."

"But this is the real thing, this works just right."

"I don't know, now . . . Lemme see it."

"Well, it ain't exactly Spanish Fly, it's something better.
We picked it up in Denmark. I'll put some in your beer."

"Hold on, hold on," said Jack, putting his hand over his
beer glass. "Now I don't want to try none of that foreign
stuff. I ain't sayin' it'll work, but if it does then it ain't
for me. From what I heard you take that stuff and you go
right crazy, runnin' after dogs and cats and anything in
sight, climbin' onto fire hydrants, lampposts, anything, and
you can't stop for days. Either way, I don't want it."

"You got it all wrong, old man. You been hearin' wild
stories from guys who don't bloody know what they're
talkin' about. Anyway, this stuff is mild, all it does is get
you up and you get real horny and you'll give your wife a
nice time. And it only lasts about an hour, two at the most.
We all tried it. We wouldn't give you something that's gonna
cause you harm."

"I don't care. Thanks all the same, but I gotta watch me
health at my age."

"Waiter, bring us another round," said one of the sailors.

About an hour and a half later Jack was saying, his voice
a little thick, "Now you're sure this stuff works, you ain't
tryna make a fool of me, I mean what's it like again?"

For the tenth time the sailors explained the joys and
glories, the wildest sex pleasures that a man got when he
took their love potion.

There's no doubt that Jack would never have taken this
potion if he hadn't got drunk from all the free beer. He
watched while they dumped the powder in his glass.
"Only a little," he said, "not too much."

"We'll just give you half a portion," they said, though

they probably gave him at least a full one, and maybe a lot more.

"Well, here goes," said Jack, and he belted the glass of beer back. He sat there a moment, working his lips, concentrating, waiting for something to happen.

"Don't taste like nothin'," he said. "Can't feel nothin' yet either."

"It takes a while. It creeps up on ya, like."

They got him another beer and he took a drink, a sort of abstract look on his face while he tried to experience the effects of the powder.

"You guys must be tryna fool me, I don't feel nothin', it don't work."

"You wait. It'll fuckin' well work." And the sailors laughed. Jack laughed too. "Might be I'm too strong for it," he said, "maybe it's like drinkin', I can handle me liquor, it don't affect me much at all."

When closing time came around, which was not long later, Jack said, "Well, thanks for the beer, me boys, and I don't know about that other stuff."

"You'll see when you get home."

"Could be I'm startin' to feel a bit horny now. I better get movin'." He stood up, weaved a bit, then said, "Ya know, I do feel a bit funny, come to think of it. No foolin'."

The three Limeys laughed, coughing on their beer.

"Watch out for stray dogs, old man, and don't rape no bloody fire hydrants."

Well, old Jack staggered out of the Black Horse and along Water street and down by the railroad station, which was the direction he took to get home. It was a fine summer night, mild and starry, and the station was by the river and the waves slopped up against the wharves. Jack followed the track along side the old log boom that wasn't used anymore. His house was about a quarter mile up the track and overlooking the river. He was drunker than normal

because as long as the sailors were paying for the beer he
had made a point of taking advantage of a good thing.

By Jesus, he was thinking, I can feel it sure enough, them
Limeys was right. Oh boy. He had sort of an itchy tingling
feeling at the end of his knob, an impatient kind of feeling
that something better be done about it. It was still hanging
there but he knew, he knew for certain that it would come
around readily as soon as the right occasion arose, else
why would it feel that way? An unfamiliar wave of fierce
passion or something like it ran up and down his body. It
was especially strong at the base of his spine, and in his
bowels, but the real feeling was at the end of his tool, it
was like it was itching inside. He pulled his zipper down
and rubbed at it a bit, trying to cool it down. But it had no
effect. Lord Jesus, he thought, what's goin' on? Goddammit
I'm horny, holy sufferin' Christ! That stuff was powerful.

He quickened his steps, stumbling along in the dark,
hurrying and staggering to get home. He could see the light
left on in the kitchen ahead and he panted his way almost
trotting now over the cinders beside the tracks. The waves
washed in against the track embankment but he wasn't
paying any attention to that.

"Flora for Jesus sake wake up if you're asleep 'cause
I'm comin' to get ya!" he shouted as he burst in the door.
Hopping around in the kitchen like there was ants in his
drawers he tore off his clothes, getting caught in a pantleg
and falling down on the floor, rolling around and struggling
to get those clothes off.

"What's goin' on down there?" Flora appeared at the head
of the stairs in her long flannel nightie. Her eyes popped
wide open at the sight of her husband rolling around on the
floor with half his clothes off.

"What in—have you gone crazy? What in the world are you
doing?"

"I'm comin' to get ya! Holy liftin' Jesus I'm on fire—"

Flora stared at him. She looked like she was going to
faint on the spot. One hand went to her open mouth. Her
teeth were out for the night and her little mouth was all
sucked in like an old person with no teeth, which is what
she was.

"You—you're drunk—you've gone out of your mind—"

By now Jack had everything off but his shirt and socks,
and kicking the rest of his clothes aside he staggered
sideways a moment, regained his balance, braced himself,
looked up the stairs at her, then took off at a run up the
steps. Flora squeaked, turned and ran into the bedroom,
trying to close the door behind her. But there wasn't
time. Jack pushed the door open and the next thing he had
her on the bed with her nightie thrown on the floor.

Flora was whimpering and squeaking and pushing at him
because she'd just awakened and was not in the mood for
a sexual encounter, besides being long out of practise.
The sight of Jack standing in front of her had half
petrified her. It was something she hadn't laid eyes on
for a long time, his old member pointing upwards at her
like a cucumber, bobbing up and down as he made his
way unsteadily towards her. Then it all happened in a
rush, his tearing and tugging at her nightgown and then
it was off and she was thrown on the bed and suddenly
he was all over her. He was panting and growling like
an old bear.

"Stop it," she protested, but Jack didn't hear her, he
was beyond containing himself, rummaging his face over
her body, her wrinkled old skin, her tiny breasts like two
deflated prophylactics, his big rough hand clenching a
loose handful of her buttock. In his mind now, drunken
and confused the way it was, she was Flora in her youth
again, robust and pretty and full of vinegar.

He had one breast in his mouth, practically the whole
thing, and then a strange sound, an awful moan and growl

like you might hear somewhere deep in a jungle came out
of his throat, and—though I hate to say it, but it's true—he
bit. His teeth clamped together like a vice, they were his
own teeth, strong and yellow and as good as they always
were, they came together like a starved dog sinking its
fangs into a hunk of meat.

Flora shrieked. Instantly Jack realized what he had
done. He paused. His mouth was full with a wet and
rubbery substance. With blood dripping over his lips he
turned his head and spit out on the floor.

Five minutes later he was clumsily tying a bandage on
the left side of Flora's bleeding chest. She was uncon-
scious, her face gray and shrunken, tiny whimperings
coming out of her.

When the bandage was on Jack went to the phone and
called an ambulance. His penis was still itching and
burning, even now, but he didn't feel too horny anymore,
he felt sick and bewildered.

"The wife's had an accident," he said into the phone.
"She . . . she, uh, she cut herself, I think, somethin'
happened to her . . . I don't know for sure . . ."

Well, the ambulance came and they loaded Flora into it,
and Jack stayed at home while they took her to the
hospital. He wondered why the ambulance guys had stared
at him so oddly. Then he went into the bathroom and
noticed his face in the mirror and the blood on his stubbly
chin whiskers.

Despite her age, Flora survived all right, they sewed up
the place where her old breast had been, but she wasn't
hesitant about telling the people at the hospital what had
happened.As a result a couple of policemen came to Jack's
place and took him off to jail.

He wouldn't say anything that night about what had

happened. He was too embarrassed or ashamed or confused.
He just wouldn't say a word. He went to sleep in his cell.
The next day they got the story out of him.

"You know, I was thinking I dreamt it," he said. "I woke
up and I remembered a terrible dream, a regular nightmare,
and I thought my Jesus that's an awful thing to dream about,
and then I noticed that I wasn't home but it looked like I
was in jail. I thought first I'd got too drunk and that's
what'd happened, they'd got me staggering around the streets
or into some mischief. So to straighten myself out I began
going over what I remembered of the night, and I remembered
these sailors who bought me all the beer and then I realized
Holy Christ I don't think that was a dream after all. Then I
couldn't think too much more and I said to myself, I'll wait
and see what they tell me, because it's probably okay,
they'll just tell me it's okay and I'll figure out later what
was a dream and what wasn't. But my worst fears are come
true. And it ain't my fault either, it's those goddamn Limeys
who give me the Spanish Fly, and now look what happened.
You're sure Flora's all right? She ain't gonna be too happy
with me after this."

Flora wasn't too happy it was true, and for a few days she
insisted that her husband had to be put in an insane asylum
because clearly he had gone round the bend. She was told
Jack's story about the three sailors but she said at first,
"That's only a lie he made up to try and get out of it. I
never heard of such a thing." But after a while she changed
her mind. As she said, "Maybe it's true, maybe it ain't, but
maybe it is because he never done nothin' like that before.
Anyway if they put him in prison or in the asylum what's
gonna happen to me? I can't work at my age and I got the
rheumatism and that old age pension won't keep me goin',
not these days with prices what they are."

Whether what Jack had taken in his beer was really
Spanish Fly or whatever it was, the police couldn't find out,

because the pulp boat had sailed early in the morning
while Jack was still sleeping it off in his cell.

A lot of people don't believe there is such a thing as
Spanish Fly. They figure it's only something you hear about
in dirty jokes or farfetched stories. The police, I don't know
what they thought, they didn't know whether to believe old
Jack or not, and it's possible they didn't, but because he'd
been around town a long time and had never gotten into any
trouble other than a bit of hard drinking, and because Flora
didn't want charges laid they dropped the whole matter and
let Jack go.

Flora was soon out of the hospital, her wound healing very
well for an old lady like her, and they were living together
again. Jack, to show his repentance, even stopped going to
the tavern after work. At least he stopped for two days, but
he couldn't take any more than that, and the third day he
was sitting in the tavern as usual drinking his beer. But, as
he assured Flora, he would not let sailors put anything in
his beer again. When he relates his story to guys at the
Black Horse, and he doesn't mind telling it—" . . . and I
went home, I tell ya, and I was so be-Jesus horny I bit one
of the wife's tits clean off, so help me God—" he warns the
boys to watch out for them Limey sailors and for Christsake
to keep away from the Spanish Fly because it's deadly as
dynamite.

Many people now, the guys around town, they don't call
him just Jack now, or old Jack, they call him Spanish Jack
even though he's not a Spaniard.

A cold frosty morning

JAMES JUST NATURALLY pisses
one off with his moral superiority the asshole he must
practise before the mirror looking angelic and fulfilled it's
all such bullshit—
"Like a fool I told James alright I'll go put in a few
hours at this place I'll paint some damn walls why not I'm
just as much a virtuous sonuvabitch as you it'll give me
all the moral complacency I need for two months I'll be
able to wake up in the mornings and I'll think of that good
thing I did and I'll feel like a perfectly decent human not
the crumb leaching off his girlfriend sponging all the time
scheming to get places get recognized get dozens of great
books out sometimes you wake up in the morning there's
that moment that instant it seems like so much horseshit
trifling horseshit nobody'll read it why don't I do something

useful make money raise kids or something though kids
are getting to be superfluous these days but I couldn't do
that I couldn't take a job I had jobs you get a job well
you think *this* is bad now in the morning a kept poet well
waking up knowing like there's worse yes there's when I
worked for Washburn one whole year of Washburn looking
over my shoulder trying to get more work out of me—'what!
you haven't finished this run yet—what are these spots,
that will *never* do—didn't you see the spots Brennan? It
will have to be done again—is your mind on something
else?' and all those other guys looking at me like they
knew I wasn't going to stick secretly knew I was writing
poetry on the side that I that something was missing in my
makeup and that's true whatever it might be but getting up
for work catching the bus on freezing winter mornings the
dull endless ride to work the long pointless day the tired
wasted feeling riding home the fatigue the beers the TV
the yawns the going to bed exhausted early better to get
up a poor poet living off your family or your girlfriend—
    "James of course bounds out of bed in the morning to
help the poor the phony bastard falls asleep his conscience
glowing knowing he's been selfless again it's perfect it's
perfect yes for his ego who he's helping he's helping
himself *using* these impoverished bastards using the poor
and dispossessed the worst of it is it *seems* to work though
he might be putting it on one day he'll probably jump off
the Jacques Cartier bridge why can't I be a saint myself
and have spiritual contentment? What bullshit!
    "When he asked I said the hell with that look James I'm
too busy working on my poems I don't have time for helping
out pensioners yes yes I know I should but you're better
at it than me and what can I do I'm no carpenter or house-
painter I'd only make a mess of things tell the poor I
appreciate their problems and I wish them well and if ever
I get rich you can be sure I'll pass along my money to do

my bit—well I mean what could I do he was trying to put
me on the spot with his moral pressure I told him look it's
your *business* helping them out that's your calling in life
look I can give you some poems of mine and you can read
them to the old bastards everybody's got their own vocation
as Father O'Donnell always told us—remember—'It's okay'
James says 'I'm not trying to talk you into anything if you
can't help it's alright I know you're busy and I understand
that this makes it difficult for you I won't now let's forget
about it I only thought I'd mention it I'm looking around
for some guys who can offer a little free time that's all I
can't expect everyone to volunteer but if some time you've
got a morning to spare just let me know and I'll give you
something to do there's always something some of these
people the conditions they live in as you can imagine old
crippled undernourished living in the worst dumps it's a
shame you know—'

"What would I know about painting walls? To start the
morning off there was one envelope in the mail the mailman
comes early I opened it to find four poems with a rejection
slip from a little magazine in Toronto a magazine with a
circulation of 300 and they turn down my poems with a
pretentious little letterpress rejection slip and not a word
of comment that pissed me off as if I wasn't already
      "I set out wearing an old pair of corduroys and a sweat-
shirt and my heavy cowhide coat because it was freezing
cold the snow on the ground was hard as iron Breathing
like a steam engine I took the bus at the corner of Clark
and Pine and headed west along Pine with winter people
bundled together in the seats around me the bus bulling
its way up Pine past the towers of the Royal Victoria
Hospital and falling away to the left the downtown city
buildings thrown together like windowed building blocks

Place Ville Marie the Royal Bank Building black Place
Victoria Chateau Champlain the gigantic cheese grater
others towering glass inverted mineshafts it was a frozen
blue morning and beyond the city you could see the squat
misty profile of Mont Saint Hilaire about thirty miles away—
changing
    "Changing buses at Cote des Neiges Road going down
the hill and getting off at Dorchester and Guy then I had
to take the 78 to Notre Dame still holding onto my transfer
because believe it or not I had to take yet another bus that
meant four buses it took to get me there and they weren't
just waiting for me either I mean no quick transfer like the
pony express every transfer meant stomping my feet on the
frozen ground jumping up and down waiting for my bus
staring along the street hands in pockets mouth fuming like
a dragon scowling and cursing at James the phony and
thinking I was stupid as hell to do this there are do-gooders
and do-badders and do-nothingers and I thought it was good
enough to be the last of these I didn't get any special kick
out of helping the helpless that was for certain types like
James who'd walk across the North Pole to help someone
if everyone was happy and contented James wouldn't know
what to do with himself he'd waste away from misery he
was in a sense like a doctor who profits off the disease
and pain of others or a cop or a fireman or an undertaker
if everything was going well they'd have no place in life
but why did James have to get me into this I'm the kind
born to help out by contributing money anonymously or
even openly it remained for me to get hold of the money it
was that simple all James had to do was wait a few years
and perhaps I'd get rich somehow just like that you never
could tell Meanwhile I was freezing on the corner of Notre
Dame and Guy and supposed to visit some old sonuvabitch and help clean and paint his apartment when I could
be home working on my poem my new poem—the poem that

needed so much work because it was so long for me the
slow but certain sure worker like some other good poets If
I'm slow I'm sure my poems are tight and taut—
    "The sun up bulging with brilliance but it wasn't doing
much yet to warm up the city it was nine-thirty now another
thing that rat James got me out of bed making me get out
of bed at eight oclock 'just this one day' sure but I lose
the day it upsets everything I'll be worn the hell out I know
it not able to get any work done in the evening and maybe
tomorrow probably I'll wake at eight that's the way my
body works and won't be able to get back to sleep and man
that will piss me off because I can't start work that early
waking at nine is just right I make my coffee and Diane is
already gone to work and I'm alone in the apartment it's
warm and locked in from the bitter cold outdoors so I take
my shower and make my coffee and in my old wool house-
coat sit at the desk and get myself ready get the pages out
I'm up to four pages now the longest poem I've done yet I
try to avoid thinking about outside things like and I wouldn't
admit this to anyone but when you get that far along and
you think it might be a major work little thoughts creep in
and you have to keep them out until the work is finished
because they might interfere with the flow like I'm thinking
of well I suppose I would submit this for the President's
Medal that is if I get it published but Christ surely anyone
will see Thinking too of the Tamarack might as well try it
there start at the top—my thoughts are always turning this
way except I put them out of my mind best I can when at
my desk it takes a while to get into the poem but then it
starts to come the right word the line the movement the
sound it's all got to be right Christ I must write each line
I don't know how many times it's a pursuit of perfection is
what it is and now here I am down here in the slums standing across from the Salvation Army an old tavern at my
back it's 9:30 in the morning and those guys going into the

tavern Christ it's only 9:30 in the morning two men in their thirties one with a light windbreaker on and his shirt half unbuttoned and his chest bare to the piercing air and the other guy in a dirty red and white leather jacket and high-laced work boots they duck into the tavern and across the street a couple of old women climb the steps to the Sally Ann Next time I see when I see James I'm going to tell him to go fuck himself The hairs of my nose are stiffened Stomp stomp stomp at least my feet haven't frozen yet and to make it worse I've got to buy the goddamn groceries some-time today and get that print that Diane wants when am I going to do that? I'm not going to stay down here all day fuck it I'll do my bit and clear out I think my hair is frozen dammit and that's just another thing I forgot about being out in the cold how could I forget I didn't forget I just didn't think I never go outside this early it's habit I can't start the day off without a shower and every three days I wash my hair and that's just right it works out just right and everything just moves along well I start my work fresh and when you get a working routine you can't break it especially if you're doing something of major value as I think—well no point going on about that but it pisses me off because what if today *was* the day when it all comes together how can I tell—but now yes it feels like the ends of my hair are frozen I'll probably get my hair full of fuck-ing paint too and that'll be lovely I don't know if it's frozen it's cold you can't tell and I had to sit there with Diane's hair dryer on hopping mad cursing and swearing that arsehole James why do I know guys like that why didn't I tell him emphasize how important this work was I was doing when's that goddam bus coming it's I've been standing here fifteen minutes almost and—yes there's some other bastard fuck him too another of these holy frauds I should tell him to paint the bloody place himself boy I'm seething am I pissed off I'm frozen right through—

"Minutes like hours later broad face of the bus appearing down the street coming slowly from the east it stopped at two stops moving casually along taking its time the driver getting a big kick out of the human icicles standing at the stops ahead of him There were three women and a short little man waiting with me the women began digging tickets out of their purses as the bus drew up I was there first but I let them get on ahead of me that's my good turn for the day now I can go home I was shivering and my feet had begun to get numb The windows of the bus were frosted over some of them had little peepholes where passengers had rubbed their bare hands on the frost to melt it off I figured I'd better do the same so I'd know when I got to this place some old Mr. Benoit his name crippled with arthritis about seventy years old lived by himself in some dump and James said it would help to clean it up and paint it there was going to be another guy there graduate student McGill not much of an apartment said James hardly more than one room in fact just a tiny room with a tiny kitchen and bathroom the old man neither drank nor smoked James said he couldn't afford to he'd been living there about fifteen years all by himself and the apartment had deteriorated if it was ever anything to begin with and it probably wasn't—'just clean it up and paint it' says James 'how long will it take?' I say 'I never painted anything in my life' 'well John will show you he's into social work of course he'll show you like he can get it started while you're doing some cleaning he has the stuff he'll have all the equipment there' 'it sounds like a lot of work' I say 'no it won't take long a matter of hours just dig in and get at it a matter of hours' 'well if that's all . . .'

"The bus took its time passing the little grocery and beer stores and taverns and hole-in-the-wall snack bars and rundown old brick buildings and ragged kids out playing in the sidestreets I checked the piece of paper again with the

address and directions and when I got close I pulled the
cord and got off at the approaching stop I had to walk half
a block then cross the street and go down a sidestreet a
ways to get to the place

"A few low crumbling attached buildings squeezed in
between a black warehouse and an old ironworks factory
the factory sombre and sitting there between owners or
waiting to be demolished the other side of the street a long
high wooden fence bore the sign Creary's Lumber Yard the
street ran one-way for a block and at its foot or head traffic
was speeding by the old guy's address one of the squat
little buildings seedy brick front marked over by kids with
crayons and chalk a motheaten brown curtain showed
through the frost on the ground floor window no other
curtains in any other windows I could see I walked past the
house cars parked both sides of the street looking for the
panel truck this John was supposed to have driven here I
looked at my watch it was five to ten I was five minutes
early but I'd assumed the bastard would be so keen to help
the needy he'd be here ahead of time and have the work
half done well now what the bus ride hadn't taken the frost
out of my bones I stood on the sidewalk shivering then
walked back boots squeaking on the hard snow I looked
at the house there it was so what do I do now go in and
start sweeping floors where is that prick maybe he didn't
bring the truck he might've come in a car or maybe he
parked somewhere around the corner or in an alley the
rotten bastard I should have worn a heavy sweater I can't
stand out here all day maybe the old sonuvabitch'll give me
a cup of coffee maybe that John character is already in
there that'd be great now if I stood out here freezing to
death waiting for him and he was inside all the time—
"I approached the door tried to look in through the glass

it was covered with thick furry frost and I couldn't see a
thing no bell so I knocked I knocked gently I had no gloves
on I'd kept my bare hands in my pockets the paint on the
door was rough and jagged I was afraid to rap on the frosty
glass for fear it would break I hammered the side of my
hand like a karate fighter against the door it was like
beating on rough cement No reply I tried again forgetting
and using my knuckles and tearing the skin icy air biting
at my bare hand once more hand like brittle china I hit at
the door A thought jumped into my head—I could go away
now he wasn't home I'd tried done my bit I'd showed up and
almost tore my hand apart and the old man that I was trying
to help was away somewhere he probably didn't want help
he was too proud so he just locked his door and went out
to visit a friend or something I could be as indignant as
hell with James look here man you get me out of bed early
and out in the cold and I show up and not only is your friend
John not there but there's nobody home 'But he *was* home'
I could hear James saying 'and John got there on time at
ten'—'Like hell he was there there was no truck and I was
at the place at ten (I looked at my watch one minute to if I
took off now I don't want to run into John just showing up
as I'm leaving) and that old guy I knocked and knocked and
almost knocked the door down and broke my fist almost my
knuckles are all bloody if he was there why didn't he
answer I almost froze to death I couldn't stand around all
day at his door I must've been ten minutes trying to get in
but nobody answered I figured he'd forgot about us coming
or didn't want us so he was either out or in there hiding till
I went away I got frozen stiff and I wasn't going to wait
around for your friend John if he was on time then either
his watch or mine wasn't working right so I said what the
hell I was really pissed off I went all that way to help some
old fucker and I was just wasting my time'—'But I'm telling
you he was there he just didn't hear your knock he's an

old man his hearing's not good John's there now he called
me about noon wondering where you were I know you can't
go down now—' 'you're damn right I can't'—fuming and
sounding outraged as hell—'I'll talk to John this evening
and find out how he got in he didn't mention any problem I
wonder what happened I'll call you after I've talked to
him'—'maybe the old man came back from wherever he was
or woke up or something I don't know anyway all I know is
you just look at my hand if you don't think I knocked hard
enough.'—

and later James calls again and says I talked to John and
he says you must have been knocking at the outside door
because there's a little hallway inside and the old man's
apartment there's two apartments in there one unoccupied
and the old man's and there's two inside doors . . . I didn't
know that how could I the window was covered with
frost . . . didn't you try the outside door? it was open all
you had to do was turn the knob and walk in and knock at
the inside door . . .

I looked down at the knob I looked up the street but no
panel truck coming it was ten o'clock.

'John said he might've been one or two minutes late
because of the traffic but not more'—

One or two minutes maybe one minute If that door was
open I could turn the knob and then well I've got a
conscience I mean I believe the old man's not here or
doesn't want us I mean that's a legitimate reason for not
hanging around but if this door if it's locked well hell that's
it I mean that's it I'm getting the hell out of here But if
it's open—'well I never thought of trying the door it never
occurred to me it looked locked I mean you don't just walk
into someone's place like that I was thinking it was his own
door it looked like it the place was only small I didn't
think there'd be more than one apartment there why in fuck
wasn't John there on time or even early he should've known

I don't know anything about this kind of stuff'—

"I was shivering and feeling a rotten anticipation of going
inside and grubbing around cleaning up some filthy hole
why in hell I mean that's a government thing that's why
social agencies exist that's *work* employment for some
people everyone complaining about unemployment and now
they expect me for nothing to go clean up some lousy
apartment that should be torn down not cleaned up or else
fixed up by someone who knows what he's doing and getting
paid for it Christ I write poems that's enough work to do
for free now I'm supposed to go cleaning up the slums
while the fat fuckers in the government drive their limousines
and pad their bank accounts in Switzerland what in hell are
taxes for?

"I started to break away and take off the urge was almost
irresistable because time was flying and that panel truck
any minute might come and this last escape route would be
closed look at that frost in the windows not only the door
window but the front window off to the side that house must
be like a deep freeze inside I can see me scrubbing floors
and painting walls with my big coat on bloody misery Okay
I know that old guy lives in it all the time but that's the
system it's got to be fixed up here I am I'd just be
perpetuating it by contributing the minimum aid keeping the
important and necessary things from getting done that's a
social problem that has to be legislated against I don't
want to be like some nobleman coming down to the poor
once a year pretending to help them and getting a good
feeling that doesn't help it only allows these conditions to
exist I shouldn't be here I'm never going to thaw out—

"I put my hand on the doorknob Surely to God he wouldn't
leave his front door open if it wasn't open—my heart stepped
up its beat the street was there one-way south I would walk
briskly because I had to get warm find a little restaurant
and have a coffee and thaw out then take the bus uptown

and do that shopping and get home and see what could be
salvaged from a fruitless adventure—

"The knob turned and the door opened My spirits straining
to make a getaway down the street were stunned sunk to
the ground at my feet Oh Jesus Christ I'd forgotten almost
that I might actually do that shit I'd come to do I'd almost
got out of it my resolution had been crumbling away in the
face of a way out oh hell I could still close the door I stuck
my head inside it was dark as night suddenly the stench
hit me like a fist in the face it was as if the floor was
covered with decaying bodies or decades of garbage was
piled up pulsating with maggots in the cold air the odor
was petrified and ghastly something scurried across the
floor like a shadow in the dark I closed the door again
something I remembered a thing I'd read in the paper in the
summer some highschool kids with a grant from the
government to go into the slums and help out the poor not
unlike what I'd set out to do and the kids said they were
amazed at what they found that one place they went the
apartment was crawling with cockroaches they were like a
moving carpet on the floor they were all over the kitchen
table and the sink and the dishes and the old couple who
lived there when they ate the roaches crawled all over the
food and they just shook them off before taking a bite this'd
be the same thing this is the kind of rundown dump and it's
an old man with no hope for a long time and the wildlife of
the slum has taken over and was I supposed to go in and
confront cockroaches and rats and mice and spiders for a
day in the middle of the freezing cold of winter—I jumped
when the rat or mouse crossed the hall floor jumped with
fright and repulsion and the smell almost made me gag I
knew by God this wasn't the place for me I'd think about it
later but my reaction was so immediate that you couldn't
say I thought about it then my entire body my spirit they
just reacted together my brain hardly had a say at all or

else I might have stopped and reasoned matters out and
made a more noble and self-sacrificing decision whatever
it might be but one instant of total revulsion closed the
door and saw me take a quick glance up the street and a
look at my watch one minute after ten well John wasn't
showing up and I'd knocked hard and I was beating a
retreat down the street walking on the verge of running
Near the corner I gave one look around I had to know if the
panel truck had arrived and seen me I couldn't explain
myself if it had but it wasn't there never mind if that was
it nosing around the corner back at Notre Dame I'd made my
turn now still walking rapidly out of sight of the street an
enormous sense of relief mixed with a few other feelings
but when you thought about it I was right I'd do what I could
when the opportunity presented itself in the future press for
sweeping social reform you had to do these things from the
top for me to paint some cruddy wall wasn't the answer.''

College town restaurant

THE WAITRESS WAS a stout country girl. You could tell she was from the country by the way she talked, for instance she would pronounce the word "now' like "nyow", or "house" like "hyouse". Her skin was coarse and she had an eyetooth in the front of her mouth, and there was a big mole on her cheek. And yet she was not entirely unattractive.

At some point, it would be around nine-thirty in the evening, a husky fellow came into the restaurant and sat at the counter. I gathered by the way he talked that he was from the country too, and he must have been from the same place as the waitress because he knew her. He carried a visored cap in his hand and placed it on the stool between himself and me.

"You're early tonight," the waitress said. She was

washing cups behind the counter.

"I couldn't sleep. Harry brought his guitar over and they all got singin'."

"D'you want a coffee?"

"Yeah. Workin' hard tonight?"

"No."

He smiled broadly at her. She looked past him at the booths, to see if there were any unserved customers. The restaurant was packed but it would be a mistake to think a lot of money was being spent. The customers were mostly students from the highschool and the college and they put in hours over the same coffee or coke. Newbridge was a small town and the Castle Restaurant was about the only place you could go in the evening. There were more students standing around waiting to get a booth. Some of the stools at the counter were still unoccupied.

"How late d'you have to work tonight?"

"Twelve."

She got him his coffee and scribbled his bill out. She resumed washing cups.

"Yessir, they were makin' an awful racket home. I couldn't sleep to save me soul. I'll be glad when I get off this Jesus night duty."

The waitress said nothing, not looking at him. He sipped his coffee, staring all the time at her, smiling at her when he caught her eye.

"You're not sayin' much tonight."

"No."

"What's wrong?"

"Oh . . . I'm mad at you."

Catching at this bit of badinage the fellow said roundly, "Arh, now what did I do? I never did nothin'."

But she evidently lost interest before even starting.

"Nothin'," she muttered, and went for a dish towel. In the meantime another waitress came behind the counter

and filled four glasses with coke at the fountain. She
placed them on the counter and wrote out the bill.

"How are *you* tonight, dear?" the fellow boomed, his red
face looking eagerly at her.

"I'm fine."

"Are ya workin' hard?"

"Oh yes, I always work hard." She was a blonde girl of
seventeen and talked as if she had adenoid trouble. The
first waitress returned with her towel.

"We either work hard or we go," she said.

The blonde girl clutched the four glasses in her hands
and left. The other waitress dried the cups and placed them
on a tray. When they were all dried she set the trayfull on a
shelf and stood facing the huge mirror behind the counter,
touching her hair into place. I saw the face of the country
fellow beside me beaming, and he smiled widely—his eyes
were fixed on the girl, but her face in the mirror was
passive and she seemed absorbed in her hair. A college
boy sitting further down the counter shouted, "Quit looking
at yourself in the mirror!"

The waitress flushed, and turned her head to him with a
laugh. "What?"

"Don't be looking at yourself in the mirror."

"I was just seeing how bad I looked."

"Oh. That's all right then."

The waitress went down among the booths and came back
with an order. The coffee was almost gone, and she put
another pot on to percolate. Then she poured the last two
cups from the old pot, put four lumps of sugar and a little
bottle of cream on each saucer, and carried them to a booth.
When she came back the big fellow leaned toward her and
said, "Unh—" like he was trying to start a sentence but
didn't know what to put in it. She looked at him impatiently.
"What?"

He strained toward her a moment, and said, "Unh—"

She looked at him and went about her work. Then desperately he said, "That Lena's some crazy, eh?—"

He picked his cap up and slid onto the stool next to mine, closer to where she was bent over her dishes. "We had the guitar there—she got up to sing a song—" He stopped, hesitating.

The waitress said nothing, left her dishes, and without looking at him went to the other end of the counter to putter around. I felt the man still straining toward her, half off his seat, and leaning hugely over the counter. The restaurant was full and noisy with talk and the jukebox was playing. Nobody paid the least attention to anyone else. After a while the waitress came back and said to me, almost angrily, "I gave you your coffee, didn't I?"

"Yes, this was it here," I said, nodding at my empty cup. I was using the saucer for an ashtray. I revolved around on my stool and looked down at the booths for a few minutes. When my cigaret was down to a butt I stepped on it and paid my bill and went home.

The janitor's wife

IT IS NOW February. I hate my job. I hate the place I live in. I dream of sunny Spain, of palm trees, sitting in cafes drinking cheap wine, good wine but cheap. Since I have to be frugal I've been living in an awful basement room on Saint Jacques near Atwater. My building is in a row of gray tenements which look much better outside than they are inside, though they don't look so great outside either. I get this room for $7 a week, it comes complete with fridge, sink, cockroaches and crazy people. The man next door is an insane drunk who a few nights ago chased his wife out into the snow in her night-dress. Two cops brought her back and did their best to smooth out the family quarrel. Then there's the janitor and his wife. But never mind. When you're saving money you're supposed to put up with this kind of thing. I'm not sure if it's really that much of a saving. I've gotten so I drink myself numb every night in order to tolerate the roaches and everything else about this depressing place and though I buy the cheapest wine it still costs money. I've been thinking of moving.

This is a story about a girl named Irene. Irene works in the office of the paint plant where I'm a lab technician. I make sixty-five a week.

Irene is quite pretty, she's got a big set of. . . breasts. A big set of tits. Her legs are a little heavy but you don't notice that.

I myself am not such a badlooking fellow and I am hardly what you'd call stupid. I know a few things and I've also got a sense of humour. But—I think this is the worst fault in the world especially when it comes to getting women— I seem to be very shy, very shy and self-conscious. I think I was born that way. I act like a bumbler and a stumbler, you know, and I have a hard time looking a girl or anyone in the eye, and I blush easily, and I never know what to say. I could be exaggerating this but if I'm not all that bad I still *feel* that I am. I know it shows too, I can tell by the way people look at me.

Irene is the opposite, she's easy mannered and unself-conscious and friendly with everyone—and it's because of that I thought we might hit it off. She could complement me, so to speak, make all the small talk, see that there were no embarrassing silences, help me make my moves when I was too timid. I didn't come right out and think this, but as I see it now that's what I was looking for.

Not such a long time ago she said, "Hi." She was still at her desk cleaning up and I was leaving for home, walking through the office.

"Hi," I said.

"Do you work in the lab?"

"Yes."

"What's your name?"

"Frankie."

"I mean your full name."

"Oh. Frankie Walsh."

She shuffled through some papers. "Here it is. Here's your T4 slips."

"Oh. Thanks."

That was our first encounter. After that she said hello to me whenever I walked by. The way her smile flashed I thought, "I think she likes me. I think I'll ask her out."

I wasn't living a total hermit's life. On weekends I'd go to a movie or a coffeehouse or a pub, sometimes I'd go with Gagnon and Smythe and get drunk, I needed some diversions like this or I'd go out of my mind. So it was not out of the question for me to take a girl out, providing she didn't have expensive tastes.

It took me a few weeks to work myself up to asking her, and when I finally did it was a miracle that I got through it. I would have changed my mind at the last second except I wasn't quick witted enough to think of an alternative reason for stopping at her desk in such a sweat. My voice was dry and shaking as I spoke. On my face was a twisted smile designed to show I was performing a a casual everyday act, my debonair smile. Of course it must have looked pitiful.

"Um . . . Irene . . . um . . . " That was the first time I'd called her by name. To my amazement she responded to it, to that peculiar sound that escaped my throat. She looked up at me smiling. "Um . . . ah . . . listen, I, uh . . . you wouldn't . . . you don't suppose . . . well, what I mean to say is, would you like to—would you come out—like to go—Friday night, come out with me?"

"Friday night?"

"Well, if you're busy, it doesn't matter—I mean—"

"Sure, I'd love to."

"Oh? Oh. Good. Listen, uh . . . we'll . . . like what would be, let's see now . . . Friday night . . . "

"Do you know where I live?"

"No—no I don't, no—"

She told me her address and said why didn't I call for her at nine on Friday night. She gave me another smile. I moved my mouth into the shape of what I supposed would be a smile of my own. I left quickly, my legs wobbling terribly, they could hardly support me.

I very pointedly avoided seeing her the rest of the week. I was afraid to risk a conversation. I didn't want to ruin things, I didn't want to be found out. It was impossible for me to act like a normal human being in front of a pretty girl.

On Friday evening it would not be so bad, I told myself, because whatever else we did we would have something to drink, and that would fortify me.

I heard her one night falling down the stairs and screaming. There was a scattering of feet in the hall and a man's angry voice shouting in French followed by heavy footsteps down the stairs. I had a pot of spaghetti boiling on the gas stove out in the hall but I was reluctant to go and check it. If I didn't it was going to burn dry. There was more activity in the hall but I couldn't wait any longer or the spaghetti would be ruined.

Just as I opened the door the janitor's wife ran past and started up the stairs. She missed a step and slid back on her hands and knees. She was wearing a sloppy nightgown and when she turned to look at me I saw her breasts swaying loosely down around her waist. She grinned at me and said something but she was so drunk I couldn't understand her. I turned off the gas and carried the spaghetti back into the room. It steamed and hissed when I removed the cover but it wasn't burnt.

The janitor's wife has a face scarred all over like a pin-
cushion. She would look all right except for this. Her features
are regular, her figure is acceptable if you don't mind long
floppy breasts, but her face skin is repulsive.

She knocked on my door one evening to see how I was getting
along. This was shortly after I'd moved in. She stepped inside
the room and pushed the door shut.

"How do you find your room?" she said. "It's a nice room,
don't you think?"

"It's all right. Except for the cockroaches."

"Cockroaches? Don't you have powder to keep them away?"

"Well, I see some powder spread around the room but it doesn't
seem to do any good. It's in the corners and there's some in all
the drawers."

"You should put some more."

"I don't have any."

She stood close to me, looking into my face. I turned away and
felt I had to keep talking. "I don't know . . . I don't like those
bugs around—otherwise the room would be fine . . ." I shrugged,
looking away from her. She moved closer.

"But don't you think it's a nice room?"

"Oh, it's fine. But . . ."

"I'll see you get some powder. Just spread it around and you
won't have any trouble."

"I don't know. There's quite a bit now and it doesn't seem to
bother them."

There was a moment of silence. I was extremely uncomfortable.
The woman smiled at me and with an effort I smiled back. Then
I thought it was better to show her no encouragement, let her see
I wasn't interested from the first.

"I hope you aren't afraid of ghosts," she said.

"Ghosts?"

"Yes."

"I don't think so. Why?"

"Because a man shot himself in this room, just about a year

ago."

"*Is that right? How'd that happen?*" *I pictured a young man in the grips of despair, down here among the cockroaches, taking a gun from his drawer . . .*

"*Oh, he was an old man, always sick, and living on his old age pension.*"

"*Oh.*"

"*Does that bother you?*" *the woman said.*

"*No.*"

"*Me either. It bothers some people. There was another man died here. A young fellow. That was two years ago.*"

"*Another one? How did that happen?*"

"*He fell down the stairs. He was drunk. He broke his neck. But he didn't die right away, they took him to the hospital. Two days later he died.*"

"*This place has quite a history.*" *I tried to laugh. I was uneasy with her eyes looking frankly at me like that. And she kept inching closer, standing directly in front of me. I looked at her and kept looking away, shuffling my feet to keep my distance.*

"*Do you feel lonely down here by yourself?*"

"*No, no,*" *I assured her.* "*I'm used to that.*"

She stood without saying anything, gazing into my face, just standing in front of me. It was obvious what she was about, it was so obvious to both of us it was farcical. I might as well have said, "*Beat it, I can't stand the look of you.*" *I certainly didn't want her. First there was her husband—that could be dangerous. But that wasn't really it. It was her face. For all she attracted me she might have had leprosy. The janitor's wife repeated herself, said what a nice room it was. I answered with a word or two, staring over her shoulder.*

"*Do you have any laundry I can do for you?*"

"*No. Thanks anyway.*"

At last she left. She smiled going out the door, but it was a curious smile, something between injury and indecision. Later

it occurred to me that she might just think me bashful. I appeared
that way, surely, with my averted eyes, weak conversation,
politeness. I wondered if she had really understood that I wasn't
interested, that was all. I watched closely next time I saw her.
Her eyes looked into mine frankly. She wasn't finished yet.

Her husband was French, a small man with bristly red hair and
a moustache. He wore a perpetual foolish smile and walked like
Groucho Marx. He could speak English only slightly and looked
the picture of helpless frustration when he couldn't find a word
he was searching for. His hands came up trying to draw the
meaning out of the air, an expression of apology, a pleading for
forbearance on his face.

Immediately after work Friday I went with Smythe and
Gagnon to Marriot's Tavern. Marriot's is in the midst of a
lot of factories and naturally does a flourishing business.
Smythe eats there every day and Gagnon who has a wife
and three small children about twice a week, but for myself
I feel I can afford it only once every two weeks, on pay day.
Other days I bring my lunch and eat it in the lab, always
the same lunch, one baloney sandwich and one peanut butter
sandwich.

Sometimes on Friday the spirit of the weekend is too much
for me. I awake Saturday morning remembering vaguely that
I stayed with the boys at the tavern and later, at some point,
we took a cab uptown and visions of shoddy nightclubs on
the Main pass through my head, bar girls and strippers and
low coloured lights, loud bands, drunken talk, and count-
less pints of beer. I examine my wallet and count the change
in my pocket, and with a little calculation discover there's
five or six dollars missing. The reason it's not more is
because of Gagnon. After a certain stage in the night it's
impossible to pay for your own drink, he insists on picking
up all bills. Once he's had a few in him he acts like a

free-spending millionaire. But I don't want to start talking
about Gagnon. Nor about Smythe who is an Englishman with
a beard. I get along pretty well with them despite the fact
I make less money and do more work.

"I've got to go," I said, after four beers. "I'm taking a
broad out tonight."

"A broad! What broad? Tell us about her," said Gagnon.

"You don't know her," I said.

"What's she look like?"

"Not bad. I've seen worse."

"Has she got a friend?" said Smythe. "I'm not doing anything this evening."

"Has she got two friends?"

"Naw, she's got no friends, she's all by herself."

"Have you gone down on her yet?" said Gagnon. He
stuck his tongue out in a point and wriggled it around. This
was an obsession of his.

Such a question made me embarrassed. Smythe laughed.

"I just met her," I said.

"Where'd you meet her?"

"Oh . . . I don't know, just somewhere, I forget."

"Ah! Ah! There's something funny here. I bet you we know
her."

"Is she from the office?"

"I don't have time for these stupid questions, I've got to
get moving." I swallowed the last mouthful of beer.

"Tell us about it Monday, we'll want to hear everything,"
said Gagnon moving his tongue around and winking.

I had about a twenty minute walk to my rooming house.
It was dark outside and a few snowflakes were beginning
to fall. I walked quickly, crossing the bridge over the frozen
Lachine Canal. My walk took me past factories and ware-
houses and rundown tenement houses, along gloomy little
streets, then over the railroad tracks and past a two-
spired church and on up to Saint Jacques.

I finished the bottle of wine and felt nauseated. With no wine left I went to bed. My head was whirling, it was as if I was riding the rim of a whirlpool. I lay on my side breathing deeply, trying to keep from vomiting. I was sinking, sinking, sinking—

I was awakened by a pounding on the door. When I got to my feet I had to clutch the bedpost to keep balanced. I had difficulty standing upright, and in a crouch I went to the door. The janitor came into the room. He was speaking, he sounded drunk, of course he was drunk. I was sobered now but my head was light, my stomach threatening to rise, bending me over—

"What?"

"You want—come drink for beer?" The janitor laughed and slapped me on the shoulder. He pointed upstairs. I didn't really listen to him. I moved back to the bed and put one hand on the bedpost, supporting myself. I was sick to the stomach and my forehead was in a cold sweat.

"Do I what?"

"Drink for beer—you come drink for beer!" He put his hand on my elbow. Drink for beer? What does he mean? Does he want some beer from me, or does he want me to go upstairs for a drink? That would never do.

"Drink for beer! Drink for beer! Eh? You want?"

"Do I want to drink some beer?"

"Yeah! Come drink for beer."

"No, no . . . " I said weakly. "I have to get some sleep."
The man tried to drag me by the elbow.

"No—listen, I had some wine tonight and I don't feel so good."

"Eh? Come drink—" He was smiling, in good humour. He tried to say something further but his English didn't have the words. He just shrugged. "Come!"

I shook my head. I sat down on the bed. Another minute and I would have fallen down. It was possible I would throw up if the man didn't go. Beer—it was crazy to think of drinking beer now. I muttered some sort of apology, not able even to raise my head to look at the janitor when he left.

"You sure? Sure? Aw!" he guffawed. "Drink for beer!"

Where did he ever get that expression? At last he left, leaving the door open behind him. He was staggering. I summoned the will to get up and lock the door and climb back into bed. I lay under the blankets like a sick kitten, feebly offering myself to sleep which was not long in taking me.

It was still snowing and since I didn't want to look like a cheapskate I hailed a taxi. We were way out on Van Horne.

"Where are we going?" she said. In the back seat of the cab I felt the touch of her coat against mine.

"Oh, well, we'll go—I don't know—we'll go downtown, go to a club somewhere or something. What do you want to do?"

"Are you sure you don't have anything definite? Someplace you really want to go?"

"No, I don't think so, not that I know of, anyplace . . . We can—Oh, I don't know—we can go to the *Catastrophe* and have a beer, I mean a drink—"

"All right." Then she said, "Would you like to go to a party later? I know where there's one."

"A party? Oh, sure, fine. Sure, why not? Where?"

What if I'd made definite plans, had somewhere I'd really wanted to take her? But I didn't know what we were to do that evening. She was the first girl I'd asked out since coming to Montreal. Vaguely I thought we would visit a few clubs and drink and dance and talk and get to know each other and then I'd take her home, and who knows what then?

We were silent most of the way downtown. I was sure it wasn't bothering her, the silence, that she could make conversation if she wished or she could just as easily say nothing. I sat beside her trying to get my mind to revolve so I could think up something brilliant to say. All I could

think of saying was, "It's snowing quite hard," and I
wasn't about to say something as stupid as that. I squirmed,
wishing the taxi would go faster so we could get to the
Catastrophe and have a drink and my brain might unseize
itself. I glanced at her out of the corner of my eye, I could
make her out in the twilight of the cab, her long flowing
hair, her straight little nose, the bulge of her coat where
her breasts were. This is me here, I thought, I'm taking this
gorgeous girl out, she's with me, not with someone else.
It was almost enough to make me panic. Could I handle it,
was I capable of pulling it off, would she not realize that a
mistake's been made, that I had outreached myself, that I
was bluffing? I'll be cool, I instructed myself, I'll act cool
and possibly a little superior. I'm the one, it's *me* who's
disdained to make small talk, not her, I'm merely sitting
here with important things on my mind and the girl is of
minor significance in my life, just another pretty face that
I'm passing an evening with. It's all a matter of attitude.
    "I've never been to the *Catastrophe*," she said.
    "What? Oh. Oh, you haven't?"
    "No."
    "Well . . ." That must call for some further comment. But
what can you say? After all, she only made a statement. So
she hasn't been to the *Catastrophe*. Am I supposed to say,
"I've been there." You could take that for granted.
    "It's not bad," I said. "It's just a place." That's exactly
what it was, a place, a bar, a club. You've seen one you've
seen them all. "It's got funny pictures—drawings on the
wall," I said. But how could I describe them? I'd only begin
and then my description would break down because I don't
have the gift for describing things in a way to make people
laugh. And if the pictures were funny, then my description
should be funny. "You'll see when we get there."
    The taxi cost me two sixty-five plus a ten cent tip. Irene
didn't see my little tip, and the driver, he'd never see me

again. Two seventy-five. I ate beans and baloney every day
for a week to save that much.

The *Catastrophe* is above the Royal Tavern, you go up
two flights of steep stairs where there's a coat check and
a tray with a quarter stuck to it to show how much you're
supposed to tip. "We might as well keep our coats with us,
we'll only be here a few minutes," I said. Luckily there
was no waiter or bouncer around just then waiting to show
us to a table with his palm outstretched. Taking advantage
of the opportunity I quickly hustled Irene to a table. I
helped her off with her coat and draped it over the back of
her chair. It was dark, there were no electric lights, only
red candles in netted globes on the center of each table.
There was a low stage against one wall and on the wall
were the funny drawings I'd mentioned. They were drawings
of wierd looking people playing musical instruments, and
what made them most wierd was that they had feet for hands
and hands for feet. You'd have to see them for yourself.

A girl in black tights waited on us. "What'll you have?"
I said to Irene.

"I'd like a zombie."

I ordered a beer for myself. When the girl brought them
she said, "That'll be two fifty please."

"Two fifty?"

I paid, looking at Irene's tall fancy drink with disgust. I
wanted her to get feeling good but by God not at these
prices. It was all I could do to restrain myself from remark-
ing how much that zombie cost. What the hell, I thought,
it's only money. When I get to know her better I'll tell her
she should drink beer.

"How is it?" I said, trying to grin.

"It's good. Those are the pictures you meant," she said,
looking at the stage. "They *are* funny."

"Yeah." I made a sound something like a laugh. I took a
deep drink of my beer. I knew the beer cost seventy-five

cents, an outrageous price in itself, so that meant her drink
had cost a buck seventy-five. I vowed never to come to this
place again. I poured the last of my bottle into my glass
and when the head subsided took another big drink. It was
ice cold and punishing on the throat. I was shaking like
hell inside. I took another big drink and it was all gone. "I
think I'll have another one," I said.

"Already?"

"I was thirsty." A feeble smile. I certainly wasn't going
to wait until she was finished and order two of the same.
It wasn't economical. That zombie was the sum total for her
as far as I was concerned. As long as she sipped it slow
I could keep ordering beer and get feeling good and when
she finished we could leave.

When my second pint came I found myself nervously
devouring it rapidly again. I should have been getting
relaxed but I wasn't.

"Were you born in Montreal?" she said.

"No. Fredericton, in New Brunswick. I just came up here
in the fall. Are you, uh, from Montreal?"

"No, I'm from Winnipeg."

"Oh. How long have you, uh, been here?"

"A little over two years."

"How do you like it?"

"It's all right. I like it. There's more going on than in
Winnipeg."

"Yeah, that's right."

You can see we were doing some talking, not just sitting
there silently.

I wondered how old she was. I considered asking her, but
didn't know whether I should or not. She was probably about
twenty. I'd ask her later, I thought.

"Smoke?" I said, rattling my package open.

"Thank you." I lit it for her.

"This, uh, party, what time—I mean what time should, will

we go there? Where is it?'' She'd already told me but in my
distraction it hadn't registered.

"It's not far from here. It's on Aylmer. We can go anytime,
whenever you like.''

"Okay. There's no hurry, I suppose.''

I couldn't stop avoiding her eyes. I would look at her when
she spoke and then when I replied I would look at her arm,
or at the table, or at the next table. This is a nervous habit
of mine and I know I should do something about it. It's not
as if I don't know I'm doing it.

In the corner of the club, to the right of the stage, there
were musical instruments, a piano, drums, a saxaphone and
a bass. In a while four musicians appeared and began playing dance numbers. Several couples got up from their tables
and began dancing on the stage.

"Would you, uh, like to dance?'' I said.

"Not right now,'' she said.

"Oh? Okay. I don't feel like it now myself. I just thought
I'd ask.''

She smiled.

I ordered another beer, drank it, getting filled up with gas
inside, trying to slip out a few silent burps, and when I was
about to order my fourth I said, generously, "You must be
finished that drink by now. D'you want another one? Or
something else?'' Like, maybe a beer, I felt like saying.
But I was getting a little better now, a little more calm, a
little more powerful. I could see she'd almost finished her
drink. I could scarcely avoid inviting her to have another.

"All right,'' she said.

"The same thing?''

She thought a moment. Maybe she took pity on me. "No,
I think I'll have a gin and tonic instead.''

It turned out that she saved me fifty cents.

"Who's having this party?'' I said, shouting over the
music.

"Some friends."

"From at work?"

"Pardon?"

"Are they from at work?"

"No. I used to share an apartment with the girl who's having it."

"Oh."

The music stopped and the musicians took another break. The stage emptied, shadowy couples returned to their tables.

"How do you like working at the plant?" I said.

"It's all right. I don't mind."

"I don't like it, I mean my job. I'm not going to be there long."

"No?"

"I'm quitting in the summer. I'm pulling out."

"Oh?"

"Yeah, I'm heading for Spain."

"Spain? That sounds nice."

"I got a friend there, a guy from school. It's a great place, no snow, beaches, everything's cheap. Have you ever been to Europe?"

"No."

"Did you ever think of going?"

"Oh, sometimes, I've thought about it, maybe someday."

"I bet you'd like it."

"Maybe."

There was a change coming over me. The beer which I had throttled down was catching up with me. It may have been the dimness of the place too because I get drunk easier in a dark place. My head was starting to swim. It wasn't unpleasant but I had the sensation I might possibly lose control of myself if I didn't slow down. I suddenly wanted to say something like, "Hey, you're really beautiful!" I almost did. I caught my tongue in time. Something told me I had to think it over first. It would sound awful funny, coming from me especially. I had a strong urge to bend near her and kiss her. Her mouth looked wide and soft, her cheeks cool, smooth, her hair flowing and glittering. It would be nice to touch her. I started to move but my muscles didn't respond. Don't be a fool, something in me said. But I should, it's probably the best thing to do. But how would she react? If she pushed you away—what if she got mad? It's not wise to move too quickly. You don't want to look like you're getting drunk. I continued to look at her, the urge to hold her welling up in my chest.

"You'll have to send me a card from Spain," she said.

"Sure. I sure will." Perhaps I shouldn't have told her about Spain. She would realize now that I wasn't going to be around for long and there was no future in becoming involved with me.

"Of course I won't stay there forever," I said. "Maybe only a month or two. Wouldn't you like living in Spain? Maybe you can come over and visit me."

She just smiled.

"It doesn't make sense, you know, people are stupid working all the time," I said recklessly. "They're like slaves working all the time, they don't enjoy themselves, they're all trying to pay for houses and cars and all kinds of crap they don't need. Anybody with any brains would do what I'm doing. What do you think?"

"I don't know. Somebody's got to work. We can't all lie in the sun and do nothing."

"Yeah, well, some people like to work, they must like being slaves. But not me. You're smarter than that, I can see you're not stupid, you should go to Spain too."

She shrugged. "Really?"

The dance music started again. This time I really felt like dancing. I started to get up. "Would you like to dance?" I said.

"I think we'd better go now. We don't want to be late for the party."

"Oh. Oh, okay. That's right, the party."

As parties go it was the usual lousy way to waste time. I don't know if I've ever enjoyed a party in my life. When we got there we could hear the noise soon as we stepped out of the elevator. It was another of those eyesore highrise buildings. The hall was plushly carpeted and rock music was blasting from apartment 907 and there was a crowd of voices talking and laughing and shouting. We were let in by someone near the door. The lights were low and bodies were standing tightly together, there was hardly room to move around. Further in I saw a lot of motion where dancing was going on. The air was heavy and rank with cigaret smoke.

"Hi, Irene! Put your coat in the bedroom. In here."

We squeezed our way through an army of bodies, mostly male, and reached the relative peace of the bedroom. The wide double bed was buried under a mountain of coats. The girl who'd let us in was tiny and lively. "He's here,"she said meaningfully to Irene.

Irene flushed slightly. "This is Frankie," she said.

"Oh. Hi, Frankie." It was as if she hadn't seen me until now.

"Hi," I said, trying to find a place to put my coat where I could locate it again.

"This is Louise. We used to have an apartment together on Lincoln," said Irene.

"The drinks are in the kitchen,"

We fought our way to the kitchen where the sink was a sloppy mess of glasses and bottles and ashtrays, all kinds of bottles, Beefeater, Smirnoff's, J&B, Seagram's, Canadian Club, pints, quarts, forty ouncers, some strange rums in wickered bottles, a gallon of Australian port, a large basin of ice cubes. All the liquor bottles were opened and about half them were already empty. There were quarts of mix,

bitter lemon, coke, ginger ale, seven-up. A few sodden
cigaret butts lay at the bottom of the sink. Everywhere there
were empty beer bottles. A couple of guys in suits were
fussing around pouring themselves drinks. I looked in the
fridge, there were about eight dozen pints of Molson's and
Labatt's stacked inside and nothing else. It was the same
old picture. I was undecided whether to keep drinking beer
or take advantage of the hard stuff which I could never
afford for myself. I shut the fridge door. "What're you gonna
have?" I said to Irene. They say you aren't supposed to mix
your drinks, it will make you sick, but I don't know if I believe that. I've gotten sick just by drinking too much beer
and nothing else.

"A gin and tonic," she said.

I mixed a strong one for her and one for myself. She tasted
it, "Ooh, that's too strong. Put some tonic in it." I did.

Then we started wading our way to the livingroom. We
were crushed together going through a narrow hall and her
hair brushed my face. "Who's 'he?' " I said.

"What?"

"Who's 'he?' "

"What do you mean?"

"What that girl said, she said, 'he's here.' "

"Oh. I don't know what she meant."

Ha! She didn't know!

It wasn't too long before 'he' made his presence known,
I could tell soon as I saw him approaching. He was looking
at Irene and she was pretending not to see him. I could have
described him before I saw him, tall, easy mannered, very
smartly dressed and I suppose some people would even
consider him handsome, although it was not a word I would
use. He was a bit hawk-faced. "Hi, Irene, I haven't seen
you since . . . for a long time."

"Oh?" She had not said "Oh?" like that to me. I could
tell she was looking into his eyes. It was disgusting.

"Let's dance."

"Alright."

With only the faintest nod my way Irene moved off with
him. I clenched my drink. With slitted eyes I followed their
movement on the crowded floor. They danced closely together, they were waltzing even though the music was fast
and everyone else was wriggling and shaking and not touching. What goddamn nerve, what rotten nerve that guy had.
All she had to do was say, "No thanks, I'm with someone."
If it was only one dance even—but they stayed together for
half an hour on the floor while I stood lost on the sidelines
drinking and smouldering and feeling lousy and hateful as
hell.

She must have mentioned at some point that I was her
escort, because later he brought her back to where I was
and soulfully tore his eyes away from hers and moved on.
His glance for a moment had fallen over me the same way
you'd look at a chair.

I didn't say anything to her.

"Did you see my drink?" she said after a moment.

"No." It was on the windowsill but I wasn't going to tell
her.

"I wonder where it is."

"I imagine where you left it."

She looked at me. "Are you mad at me?"

"Me? Of course not. What for?"

"Paul . . . Paul's an old friend. We used to be quite good
friends."

"Oh?"

"I really had to dance with him, I could hardly have re-
fused."

I didn't say anything.

"I guess I'll get another drink," she said. She started
away. I stood there a second, then went after her. "I'll get
it for you," I said. What the hell, I didn't own her, she could

do what she wanted, so it was an old boyfriend, so what?
"Thanks."

I brought back her drink, getting myself another one while
I was at it.

"Let's dance," I said, when some slow music came on.
I didn't want to stand out there jumping around like a
monkey, I never dance to the fast stuff if I can help it.
Waltzing is more intimate, it makes more sense to dance
that way. The other kind of thing is like an exhibition, you
could do it by yourself, you don't need a partner.

"Okay."

I put the drinks on the windowsill near her old glass. We
edged our way onto the floor and—and to be blunt it was
like dancing with a post, she stayed stiffly away from me
and I almost strained my arm keeping her as closely as I
did. I felt her hair on my face but not her cheek. Her large
breasts touched against me and for a moment I started to
get a little excited but it took me no more than a moment to
sense her remoteness from me, and the stirring subsided. I
didn't say anything to her. I would have had to shout anyway
because of the volume of the music. When it ended whoever
was handling the records put on some ear-splitting screaming
and shouting by the Grand Funk Railroad or someone and I
said, "The hell with that." She stood there looking at me
quizzically, all she could see was my mouth moving. I made
a gesture of resignation and led her off the floor. "I don't
dance like that very well," I shouted at her. "It's too fast."

Then some other creep came over and asked her to dance.
She looked at me this time, she probably didn't know this
guy, and I shrugged. She went onto the floor and the two of
them were soon squirming and shaking like all the rest of
the couples. She was laughing and seemed to be enjoying it.
I had, I suppose, a kind of envy of them all out there.
They weren't selfconscious about their movements or the
expressions on their faces. "A bunch of dummies," I said

to myself. "I really hate these parties. I'm gonna leave soon even if I have to go alone. The hell with her."

"Do you like these parties?" I said when she returned.

"I guess so. Sure."

"They bore me. I find them a pain in the ass."

She didn't say anything.

"Do you want to stay long?"

"Why, don't you?"

"Naw, I don't think so. I don't know anybody here. It's too crowded, it's too smokey, it's too noisy. These parties are all alike. When do you want to leave?"

"I don't know. Whenever you like."

"Okay. Let's finish our drinks and go. We can go down to the Swiss Hut, it's only down the street."

"No, I'd rather go home."

We went into the bedroom and dug out our coats. Suddenly she dropped hers and said, "Just a minute, I'll be right back." She disappeared through the door. I stood there with my coat in my hand. Then I put it on and waited. I went to the bedroom window and looked out. In the night the city lights were everywhere, we were up high enough that you could see quite far, apartment buildings lit up, streetlights, car lights, skyscraper lights, lights on the Jacques Cartier Bridge, everything but stars. "What's she doing?" I wondered. I thought she was going to the bathroom but surely she had enough time by now . . . It was hot standing there with my heavy winter coat. "Christ!" I was getting mad. I squeezed my way out through the bedroom door to look for her. It was difficult to pick someone out in the dim light and with so many people jammed together. I pushed between bodies squeezing by like I was made of elastic. All that effort for what? In a little open space in the corner of the room that guy with his arms around Irene, the two of them clinging together like long lost lovers, and they were kissing. Never mind. I bulled my way back to the bedroom

pushing people out of the way, then in the bedroom I
decided to leave by myself and started out again. No, that
wasn't the thing to do, I couldn't run off like that, what
would I say when I saw her at work? When she asked me
where I went, and why, what could I tell her? What if word
got around to Smythe and Gagnon? In the sober morning I
would look ridiculous. The night had to end on better
terms, preferably on my terms. If nothing else, if there was
only some way I could humiliate her . . . A crazy thought
like that going through my head. In a sense I felt quite
capable now, quite strong, there was no danger of my being
selfconscious, I was too burned up, I didn't need to make
a good impression, there was nothing to be gained and
nothing to be lost. Finally she returned, flushed and
breathless. "I'm sorry I was so long," she said.

"I'm leaving now. Are you coming or staying?"

She gave me another one of those quizzical looks. As
though it was *me* who was behaving oddly. Here she was
making a fool out of me, treating me like an idiot, and when
I didn't like it she acted as if I was being abrupt and sullen
for no reason in the world.

"What do you mean?" she said. "Of course I'm coming.
I just wanted to say goodbye to Louise." Goodbye to
Louise, it was.

"Yeah. Well let's go." She put her coat on without my
help which I didn't offer.

Outside the snow was still falling, but lightly. We plodded
along the unplowed sidewalk to Sherbrooke street. I don't
know why I didn't say, "We're taking a bus, I've already
spent enough tonight." Or I could have said, "Look, it's
your turn to pay the taxi, I paid it getting here." It shows
a character deficiency on my part that I didn't have the
nerve to refuse to pay for another cab. Already I'd spent
over ten dollars. And what did I stand to get in return?

In the taxi, after all this time, she began chattering away

without a break about what a good time she had, how many
people were there, what her friend Louise was doing, where
they'd met, things they did together, mutual friends they
had, what these friends were doing. Every now and then as
she talked she clutched my arm to emphasize a point, or
when she said something she thought was funny she leaned
against me and laughed. For a long time I didn't say
anything except a bored "yeah" every so often, but she
seemed in such good spirits and she was no longer ignoring
me . . . perhaps . . . slowly and gradually . . . well, I
suppose I shouldn't be so narrow and stubborn about things,
a little thing like her kissing an old boyfriend. If I had an
old girlfriend it might be nostalgic to kiss her when we met
after a long time, there'd be nothing wrong in it. I began to
thaw. I could be big about things, forgive quickly. After all
it was *me* she was going home with, if there was anything
more to it she'd have stayed at the party and let that tall
creep take her home. I reminded myself that you can't
expect to win a girl all at once, she *knew* this other guy a
lot better than she knew me. But that was in the past.

   The meter in the front was ticking and the nickles were
adding up. But I had thrown away so much money now a
little more was almost painless. I decided on a daring
move. She was chattering and we were sitting close
together, our coats touching. Go ahead, go on, I urged
myself. Although I was fairly drunk I had still not lost
my inhibitions. Nothing ventured, nothing gained. What's
there to lose? Like a plunge into cold water I jerked my
arm up from beside her and put it around her shoulders. I
pulled her closer. She didn't resist. There was a sudden
halt in her talking but she picked it right up. I was so
concentrated on what I was doing I had no idea what she
was saying. I almost burst with triumph. My impulsive move
made me giddy. I said, "Is that right? That's very funny.
Ha ha," you know, I became responsive and started

chattering and laughing myself, almost giggling, I think.
Oh boy. I wondered if she was the kind of girl—what was
this thing I read, some psychologist, who said "not so
long ago when a boy took a girl home they kissed goodnight
but now they make love." I thought of Gagnon and Smythe,
if they could see me, see what I had my arm around. I must
have really been drunk because one minute I was sitting
glum and sulky and the next I was talking and laughing
and in my mind thinking how I was going to go about
seducing the very girl that I'd been hating so much. You
see, it was all because of the way she acted, the moment
she was nice to me and appeared to notice I was there
beside her I became a warm, generous person. It doesn't
take much with me. I thought of her taking her clothes off
and my heart almost stopped, then it began racing. Could
I do it? What approach would I take? How were these things
done? "Well, let's go to bed," the offhanded approach? Or
more romantic, "Irene darling I want to make love to
you"? I couldn't picture myself saying that. Maybe she
would take care of everything, perhaps she'd say, "Well,
let's go to bed", or "Do you want to make love to me?"
Oh yes, do I ever. Ah, I know, at least it would be the best
way, when we got to her apartment she would say, "Just
a minute while I slip into something more comfortable,"
and when she returned from the bedroom she'd be wearing
a sheer negligee that revealed everything. Just thinking
about it was almost enough to make me faint. I squeezed
her shoulder, certain that my passion was running like
electricity through my hand and into her body. She would
sense it, she would respond with her own passion. If I
were holding her hand she could squeeze back, but it was,
harder to tell with her shoulder, particularly with her
winter coat on. I looked at her profile. She became silent
for a moment looking straight ahead. I squeezed her
shoulder again. She turned her face and smiled.

When we reached her building I paid the driver, hardly
noticing the fare. With trembling hand I tipped him a
quarter, eager to get out of the car, throwing my money
away, not caring about material matters on a night like this.
The cab drove away. Irene was already standing in the
foyer out of the snow. I trotted up the walk and opened the
outer door and stood before her eagerly, smiling like a fool.
"Well, thanks for a lovely night, I really enjoyed it," she
said.

"Oh. Oh yeah. I, uh, I, uh—" What was this? Was she—
Was I supposed to say, "Aren't you going to invite me in?"
Was that the ritual? It must be my move. She wasn't just—

"I'll see you Monday, back at the old job," she said.

There was no time to waste. There was not even time to
think. Once she went in the door it was all over. The first
thing to do—I grabbed her by both arms and pulled her
close. My lips went for hers and when they got there her
head was turned slightly and they met her cheek. I released
her.

"I have to be getting in now. I'm really tired. Goodnight,
and thanks again." She had her key out and was opening
the door.

"But—"

"Yes?" she turned. I stared at her helplessly.

"Nothing." What could I say? Whatever I said I would
have made a fool of myself, more of a fool than I already
was. She gave me the last of her false smiles and disappeared inside. Goddammit all. I left the building, turning
towards Cote des Neiges on the chance the buses were
still running, my feet leaving a trail behind me in the new
snow. I was so mad—mad at her, mad at myself, mad at the
world in general—that I almost burst out crying. I trudged
through the snow all by myself on the street swearing out
loud the longest string of curses you ever heard, but it
didn't make me feel any better.

It was storming furiously outside. My window is at sidewalk level and every so often a pair of legs hurried by in the light of the streetlamp. The wind howled against the window and beat at it like a muffled fist.

I was there as usual, legs up on the table, glass in hand, quart of wine beside me. It was the only way I could live with the cockroaches. Cockroaches make my skin crawl, I feel about them much the way some people feel about snakes. At nights in bed I wear long underwear and a pair of socks in case they get into the bed with me. Then there are probably other reasons I drink wine but that was one of them.

Upstairs the janitor and his wife were having another party with some of their friends. Their feet thumped on my ceiling and from the general uproar it was apparent they were all drunk again.

Around eleven the janitor's wife came down. She closed the door behind her. "Are you coming up to our party?" I took a big drink of wine, a real big drink, then tottered closer to her, put my arm around her, led her over to the bed and turned the light out.

"Hope your husband doesn't come down," I said holding her in the dark. I had my hand up under her dress tugging at her panties.

"No, he won't. But don't be too long."

"No."

"Are you glad I came?"

"Yes."

"Do you like me?"

"Yes."

"Why don't you kiss me?"

I kissed her briefly and turned my head away, burying my face in the pillow. It was enough to make me puke. After our business was concluded I said, "You better get up there now, before he comes looking for you."

"The hell with him. Why don't you come up too."

"Me? Don't be crazy. Just say you tried to persuade me but I had a sick stomach from drinking and wouldn't go."

"I'll come see you again."

The actor

FRANKIE WAS BACKSTAGE of the theatre. He looked this way and that, finding the turmoil around him bewildering. Hordes of actors costumed in robes and armor, some of them carrying spears and swords, were running about making last minute preparations, there were whispered shouts and frantic gesturings. Frankie felt ill at ease.

Someone called out: "There's a case of wine over here! Frankie, d'you want a drink before going on?"

"Yes, yes!" Frankie shouted back, making his way to a little room. "Lemme at the wine. I need a few drinks."

He trailed his long maroon robe after him. A bottle of wine was waiting open. He drained it in three drinks. But that wasn't enough. When no one was looking he drank another bottle.

He looked at the second empty bottle in his hand, and threw it into a box of costumes. "Too much," he thought. "Excessive. I must be more careful."

The play was soon to begin. He didn't go over his lines, not wanting to tamper with the delicate balance he'd reached with his role the night before. It had not been easy. Last night, indeed, was the first time he had laid eyes on the lines. He had crammed desperately, then gone to bed feeling the role would flow freely from him, given the old Roman atmosphere of the stage setting, and his own complete release, his intuitive feel for the part, once on stage.

"I have only to submerge myself into that era, be the actual Lucius," he repeated to himself when doubt arose.

"Two bottles . . . I shouldn't have," he reproved himself. All that wine. He clutched his head.

He had trouble dispelling his anxiety. There was something . . . he couldn't locate the exact source of his apprehension. But it must lie in the script.

"A quick glance at the script will straighten everything out," he thought. But he didn't see one around.

"Anybody got a script?" he asked. Nobody seemed to hear him. "Got a script?" he questioned those passing by. "Got a script?"

"No, no I haven't. No script."

He kept asking, and one man in shirtsleeves dropped a handful of torn and disarranged sheets on a crate beside him. "Here's one," he said.

Frankie looked at it. It was too confusing, the pages were all jumbled up. "Thanks, but I need a better one."

To be on the safe side he would like to take a script onstage under his robe. "I know I'll do well, I'm a natural," he thought, "but there's nothing wrong with taking precautions. Otherwise I may have to . . . I may have to improvise."

He'd had a dream once, a short dream, in which he had
undertaken to act in a play. His first appearance onstage
was to be a brief improvization. He was to give the
impression of a very hungry man and then get off. When his
cue arrived he walked out into the glare of the footlights.
He had not come prepared with anything, but almost at once
inspiration struck him. Holding his stomach and grimacing,
he said: "I'm *so* hungry I could eat a fly's *kneecap!*" Then
a sudden glance above his head, eyes moving around, and
bang! he clapped his hands together. Holding a would-be
fly between two fingers and grinning slyly he slunk off the
stage looking back over his shoulder, licking his lips. It
went over very big. It was the highlight of the entire
night. Although it was only a dream Frankie's heart swelled
with pride.

In his role now as Lucius there was a dramatic death
scene with stirring lines, and anticipation of the effect he'd
create suddenly started him with a foolish joy. He could
picture it now . . . the audience in tears, every sense in
the theatre attuned to his dying moments, the profound
sympathy uniting all the people there . . . and when the
play was over the ovation they'd give him for his immortal
portrayal.

But all the same, it would be good to have a look at the
script just in case. There was something in the stage
directions he wasn't sure of and he couldn't put his finger
on what it was. At least he thought it was in the stage
directions. He knew his lines, he knew they'd come to him,
but there was something discomforting, a feeling of unease
he had.

If he could just check the stage directions . . .

Before he noticed it, the play was in progress.

He stood with the others in the wings, watching. He
couldn't understand why, but this didn't look familiar at
all. He wondered why they were acting the play without

rehearsals. Then it came to him. There had been
rehearsals. *He* was the only one who hadn't rehearsed.
He was the last minute substitute, replacing the original
Lucius who had taken sick, he was an "experienced"
actor who had played the role of Lucius before. It was a
bold lie—somehow he had brought it off—but now, all of a
sudden he felt the urge to sneak away and hide. A feeling
of terror was creeping up on him. He attempted to calm
himself. He told himself, it was the price of fame to take
perilous risks.

That he could act was something he knew. It was inborn,
a talent he possessed naturally. This at least should give
him confidence.

The director of the play was an actor himself. He had
taken on one of the major roles. An awesomely huge man
he was seated in the center of the stage on a throne. He
played the part of a Governor of the Emperor Trajan. The
play progressed . . .

When do I go on? wondered Frankie. He had forgotten his
cue to go onstage. Then the actors around him began
nudging him, and he saw the stern awaiting glare of the
Governor.

"Go ahead, Frankie," they were saying. "Get out there."

"Just a minute now." His panic was rising. "Lemme have
another drink of wine. Where's the wine?"

He made to go to the room where the wine was but they
restrained him, pushing him towards the stage.

"I need a script. Who's got a script?"

"Hurry up, Frankie."

He was on the stage. Through the lights he saw a large
audience gazing expectantly up at him. He must remember.
He tried to intensify his will.

But this part of the play didn't seem familiar. He couldn't
place it. "Remember," he thought quickly, "put yourself
into Ancient Rome and it will come automatically."

He walked before the throne. The Governor, a dominating personage, sat above him. His attendants, three toga-clad figures, stood confidently around the throne. The Governor's voice boomed out:

"Lucius, whence hast thou come at this hour?"

Frankie looked at him. That was odd. He didn't remember that. What was his line? But he must act naturally, give rein to his natural talents. What should he answer? *Say something.*

"From . . . I don't recall, sir."

His voice was meek. Certainly the audience couldn't hear him. He had his back turned, he should face the audience. Half-turning, Frankie raised his eyes, catching the puzzled and angered expression on the Governor's face.

"It does not seem rightly so, Lucius," said the Governor. "Hast thou spoken with our cousin Marcus?"

Marcus? What to say, what to say. *Say something.*

"Yes, sir."

A weak voice again.

The Governor's aides were looking at each other.

"And what had he to say concerning your designs on the Emperor's decrees?"

"Yes, sir." Barely a whisper.

The audience was dissolving into a featureless mass and Frankie thought he would fall down. Cold drops of sweat were on his face, his legs trembled. Why couldn't he remember his lines? The Governor said something else. He couldn't even hear him. He answered, "Yes, sir," standing there in a daze. Everything was blurred. Not one line had come back. An attendant spoke:

"Kind Lucius, come hither and we shall seek out Marcus. Come!"

The last word was a command. Frankie obeyed, following the attendant in defeat.

Backstage he was assailed by an angry cast. They

shouted at him from every direction.

"You ruined it—you ruined everything!"

"My God, what a stupid—"

"You idiot!"

"Why'd you do that?"

"It's a shambles! What a—"

"We oughta punch your teeth in!"

"Look what you did! D'you know what you did? It's ruined—the play's ruined!"

They had to find a quick replacement.

One of the actor's, a sneering, delicate-faced man who was playing a leading role, said: "I've *always* wanted to try Lucius. Great dramatic possibilities . . ." But he already had his part.

Frankie thought bitterly, "Yes, he can do any kind of acting, that fellow. It all comes easy to him."

They finally came up with a fat fruity little fellow, and he said he would do his best, but he'd have to take a script on with him just in case. "They found one for *him* all right . . ." Frankie was sitting on a crate, looking around at the others who turned only an occasional scornful glance his way.

From the stage the Governor was staring frozenly towards Frankie. He would say later that he, the Governor would have known better than to hire Frankie. There was an awkward waiting spell on stage when it came time for the second appearance of Lucius. Lines referring to the first appearance were still being hurriedly and amateurishly revised, and the new Lucius was almost as nervous as Frankie had been.

Ignored now, Frankie watched the play continue. His replacement, at first trying to speak from memory of what he'd heard at rehearsals, was forced to read from the script while trying to keep it hidden from the audience. Frankie looked down at the seats. There *was* no audience! The people had left disgusted . . . it was time for him to leave as well.

He got up from the crate and went out by the stage door. The night was quiet in the backstreet. He walked, not knowing where he was going, not caring.

He looked up and saw the entrance to a huge dancehall. Music blared above the sounds of the dancers. He lowered his head to continue on. A tall, hawkfaced man ran up to him from behind, catching him by the shoulders, playfully shaking him.

"Frankie, lad, how've you been? You're looking down! Have a drink! Here, have a drink of wine!" He laughed loudly.

"No, go away, go away . . ." He pushed him back. "Go away."

Bertha and Bill

BERTHA NORTHRUP IS one of the more unusual poets around Montreal. She was born without arms and does her writing and typing with her toes. A few years ago *Weekend Magazine* did an article on her with pictures of her using her feet for all sorts of things you'd normally use hands for.

Bertha's mother (who's now dead) took great pains to teach her to be self-sufficient so today Bertha is able to get along pretty much like any of us, or at least about as efficiently.

In May of last year a young poet by the name of Bill Lewis came up from Glace Bay, Nova Scotia. Bill stands an easy six-eight and weighs maybe 120 pounds and has a face covered with acne. Before coming to Montreal he didn't drink much but since the rest of us like to take a drop he started doing the same.

On a Friday night we were in a tavern. We thought we'd introduce Bill to Bertha. We left in a lively mood, arguing and singing and belching, and when we got to Bertha's place on Aylmer street she let us in, opening the door with her toes. As soon as we were settled she brought out the beer. For someone unfamiliar with Bertha it was a sight to watch her get the drinks. She took the glasses from a low cupboard and the beers from the fridge, and then popped them open with an opener and poured them into the glasses . . . all the time using her toes. Her legs were very supple and she could use her toes practically like fingers. She was fully competent and once you'd been around a while you hardly noticed that she had no arms. She sat on the couch drinking, holding the glass with one foot, and in the other foot she held a cigaret. She often wore dresses so, if you were interested in that sort of thing, you could see her panties with most of the moves she made. She wasn't really bad looking, somewhat along the lines of Venus de Milo.

Bill was quite taken with her. He stared at every move she made, his eyes bulging, hardly able to believe what he saw.

"Why, you're amazing," he said. "I've never seen anything like this before in my whole life. Where'd you learn to do all those things? Boy, that's really something." He sat there shaking his head in awe. "And you write poems. Let me read some of your poetry."

She gave Bill some of her verses to read. Most of Bertha's poems were feminine little things, wistfully romantic. "Here you are with no arms, and you write better poetry than I do," Bill said. "This is great stuff." Then he read a short story she'd written, about a flower that could walk, and he covered this with as much praise as her verse.

"I knew I'd run into talent when I came to Montreal," he

said, "but I never pictured anything like this. Boy, I've got a lot of catching up to do." While he was reading Bertha's writings he was pouring down her beer. He got settled on the couch beside her and they were soon engaged in a deep discussion. In the meantime, we were also drinking Bertha's beer, and a bottle of rum we'd brought along with us, courtesy of Richard Archangel, as he called himself. His real name was Richard Hogg, which he wasn't very fond of. Besides Richard there was Moe Caron, who didn't write poems but played drums in a rock band; Jack Pittman, a Newfoundlander who was leaving in a few days for South America, the last I saw of him; and myself, Sam McCarthy. It was a normal gathering for us guys, we sat around and got fairly loaded, and argued about one thing and another. We didn't get too much contribution from Bill or Bertha because they were too busy with their own conversation.

Later on when most of the liquor was gone we decided it was time to go.

"I'll stick around a bit," Bill said. "Bertha and I got too much to talk about. I can find my way home. This is the most interesting girl I ever met."

Bertha smiled, looking pleased, so we left the two of them together and departed.

"They make a lovely pair," Richard remarked when we were out on the street.

Evidently they did, at least for that night. A couple of evenings later Bill came to my place, and he was solemn. I was curious about what had happened at Bertha's after the rest of us left, but I didn't want to bring the subject up out of delicacy.

But since Bill didn't look like he was going to bring it up himself, I said, "Well, did you have a good talk with Bertha the other night?"

He looked at me morosely. "Don't mention it," he said.

"Why, what happened?"

"Nothing."

"What time did you leave? It was pretty late when the rest of us pulled out."

"I don't know," he said. "I guess I stayed there all night."

I was going to say "Oho!" but I didn't, because this was a case of a girl with no arms, which is not quite the ordinary situation. For instance, she was defenceless, if Bill had tried something.

"Have you seen her since?" I said.

"No."

"What do you think of her? She's quite a girl, isn't she?"

"Yeah, I guess so."

"You guess so? A couple of nights ago you were raving about how talented she is."

"Well," he said, "I was drunk."

"You don't think too much of her now, I take it."

"Listen, I was drunk," he said, obviously reluctant to carry on the conversation.

"Okay, so we'll forget it," I said. "So you were drunk, you got carried away, and no doubt you threw a fuck into her, and now you're sorry."

He jumped up, almost hitting the ceiling. "I never said that."

"All right, you didn't."

He sat down again. "I shouldn't get drunk like that," he said, looking very mournful.

"Then you did screw her?"

"Well, so maybe I did. But I was drunk as hell. In the morning I didn't know what had happened or where I was. I thought I was in a nightmare. I got nothing against girls with no arms, but it gave me an awful shock. I don't think I want to think about it. She called me up today and wants me to come over and see her. I told her I couldn't make it.

I don't want to get mixed up in this."

I could see he was very much bothered about it, not only about sleeping with Bertha, but because he wasn't big enough to be able to take it in stride. It was obvious he felt he was being prejudiced. I said:

"So what's wrong with Bertha? She mightn't have any arms but she's a nice girl, and she's not bad to look at either. Why don't you go see her tonight?"

He sat there with a long face, his shoulders slumped.

"I know. That's what I should do. You're right," he said. "But I don't want this to go any further. I don't want to get messed up in some kind of relationship with her. You don't know what it's like because it's not you that's involved. You can sit there and be big about it but you haven't slept with her."

"How do you know?" I said.

"Well, did you?"

I admitted I hadn't, but told him it didn't matter. I said he'd done Bertha a fine service, because it wasn't that easy for her to get a man. On top of that, I said, he'd probably done himself a service, because despite the fact she had no arms Bertha was probably good tail.

"It's only prejudice that stops other guys from getting some good sex from a real nice girl," I said. "I'd go after her myself if I didn't already have a woman."

"Yeah, sure."

"Well, why not? Nobody's ever said Venus de Milo's not an attractive woman. She doesn't have any arms. Moreover I don't think Bertha's interested in me. You're the first guy I've seen that she really took to."

He looked at me suspiciously. "What are you trying to do, anyway?"

"I'm not trying to do anything. I just think you're a pretty phony poet if you've got prejudices against a handicapped person."

"It's not prejudice. I'm not prejudiced against anybody.
I'm not prejudiced against elephants but I don't have to
sleep with one, do I? You're taking this all wrong, that's
all. You can sit there and look liberal and charitable because it doesn't concern you. But you didn't sleep with
Bertha."

"Wasn't it good?" I said.

"Well, it wasn't bad, except she had her feet up around
my face and was running her toes through my hair, and that
was a bit strange. Jesus." He shook his head. "I don't
remember anything very well because I was so drunk. I
was going like an old stallion and she was wriggling and
twisting around like a worm. I hardly knew where she was
half the time. You know what I'm like, long and gangly,
and she's pretty small anyway aside from having no arms.
After we finished she started crying for some reason, but
she stopped after a while and seemed in good enough
spirits. Then we went to sleep. I suppose I said all kinds
of idiotic things to her though I can't remember what they
were. When I woke up I had my arms around her. My head
was pounding and my mouth was dry and I felt just
miserable. I looked at the girl I was holding onto and I
couldn't believe my eyes. For about three minutes I couldn't
remember the night before and I thought I was going crazy.
I was brought up in a pretty ordinary family where everybody had all their arms and legs and you didn't think
about having sex with anyone, let alone a freak. Now, I'm
not calling Bertha a freak, because I don't think that way
now, but when I was brought up a girl with no arms was a
freak, and soon as I woke up and looked at her, that was
my natural thought. I tried to collect my wits, though I
could hardly think of anything because my head was in
such bad condition. And then Bertha woke up. Well, I
remembered then about the previous evening, and I did my
best to carry things through. I complained about how bad I

felt and she jumped up and said she'd get me a coffee. So I got out of bed and washed and got dressed and went into the kitchen where she was making coffee with her toes. You know, pouring the water and putting in milk and sugar and stirring it. Boy, just think now, how strange this was." Bill was staring at the wall all the time he was talking. He looked over at me, then looked back at the wall. "Okay, so I gulped down some coffee and then I said I had to leave right away. I had to go see somebody, I said. She saw me to the door and I got out of there, and when I hit the pavement I was some glad. I wanted to get away from that place and forget about everything. I felt lousy all day, afraid she'd feel she had some hold on me, and that she'd be expecting me to take this thing further. I felt I'd got into something. It wasn't good, that business, but it might be all right if it blew over and nothing more came of it. But then she called me today and asked if I'd like to come and see her. What am I going to do? I don't want to hurt her, and I don't like myself for not going to see her, but just the same . . ."

He was clearly in a worried state. I offered him a beer but he said he didn't want to drink anymore, not for the time being at least. He said he was thinking of going back to Nova Scotia. I told him matters weren't that serious, that he could be friends with Bertha without getting involved in a serious relationship.

"What if she's pregnant?" he said. "I didn't have any safes with me and I was too drunk to care. I doubt if she's on the pill. I mean, I'm pretty sure she's not."

"Well, that could turn out to be a problem, but hope for the best," I advised.

He went away, as disconsolate as ever. As he left I recommended that his experience might prove valuable as material for a few good poems later on, but he just looked at me. He wasn't in a poetic frame of mind.

Later on, as I was having a beer and waiting for Diane, my girlfriend so to speak, to show up—we were going to some movie or other—the phone rang. It was Bertha.

"Have you seen your friend Bill lately?" she said. I had the usual mental picture of her holding the phone in her toes, it was hard to get away from.

"I was talking to him for a while earlier," I said.

"Did he say anything about me?"

"Well, he did mention that he'd stayed at your place the other night," I said.

"Is that all he said?"

"More or less. That about sums it up."

"He was awfully drunk."

"Yeah, he doesn't hold his liquor too good."

"He wanted to stay the night, so I let him. I don't think he could have gotten home by himself. He certainly does rave on, once he gets talking. Do you think he has the makings of a poet?"

"I don't know. Some of his things look promising, but I can't say. We'll have to wait and see."

"I hope he does have some success. He's something like Alexander Pope in reverse, don't you think? He's so long and skinny and he's really not very handsome. His face is in quite bad condition. It's terrible the way acne affects some people. I feel sorry for him, don't you?"

"I haven't thought too much about it, but I suppose he's got some things working against him."

"He lives by himself in a little room, he said."

"Yeah, he's got a place on Jeanne Mance. It's pretty small, but it's cheap. He can hardly lie down in it without bending his knees."

"That's too bad. It must be hard for him, coming to Montreal after living in a small town with his parents. I feel a little sorry for the guy."

"He'll make out. He's not too helpless."

"But we should do what we can to make him feel at home here. I know if I was a stranger in Montreal I wouldn't know where to turn."

"Well, he'll get used to it."

"I called him today and asked him over, but he said he was busy. I don't think he really was, but he's a very shy boy. He practically stuttered over the phone. And you should have seen him when he left here the other morning. He hardly said a word, and he kept looking at the floor, and he hardly knew what to do with himself. I don't think he makes friends easily, and it would be nice if we could help him along."

"He's not in that bad shape, Bertha."

"Well, how would you feel if you looked like him and had to walk down the street? I'm sure people stare at him. He's probably very sensitive. He must be or he wouldn't be a poet. I probably sound like a mother hen or something but I'd like to help him along if I can. You should too. The next time you see him tell him that any time he wants to come over and talk about poetry or anything, that I'll be glad to see him. And be sure to invite him to your place as often as you can. Okay?"

"All right, Bertha. I'll do that."

But I didn't see Bill for a while after that. He kind of dropped out of sight for a while.